SEVENTH SENSE

THE CLEANSING: BOOK 1

ROBERT A. BROWN
JOHN WOOLEY

EBook ISBN: 9781386191285

Print ISBN: 9781948263290

First edition by Babylon Books

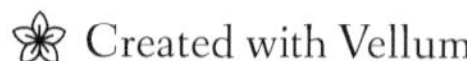
Created with Vellum

For our wives, Hattie and Janis, who have always been there for us
—and with us

May 6, 1939, Saturday night

Dear John,

I am here at last, and you and Lovecraft would love this burg. Dark, green, wet, and full of shadows. I kind of figured this would be Dust Bowl country, but I guess that's farther west, because I saw lots of streams and rivers and ponds as we came through the Ozark Mountains (which are actually "dissected plateaus," elevated places eroded over the centuries until they look like mountains – something I wouldn't have known if I hadn't picked up a book on the Ozarks to read on the train. I figured I needed to know something besides what we saw in that cornpone Republic hill-billy picture Down in "Arkansaw" last year. Remember?).

Although the first part of the trip, from St. Paul clear through most of Missouri, went smooth as silk, the last few hours of the trip were pretty rough. When I changed trains at Springfield, I got on a "mixed local" – you know, one that had both boxcars and old Pullman coaches – and it stopped at every little jerk-water town between there and here, dropping off freight, picking up cars, and pulling into sidings to let every other train on the line pass us.

I shouldn't complain, I guess. It was cheap, so I saved a little out of the travel money Uncle Sam handed me, and the seat was comfortable enough. There weren't many passengers, at least not at first, so I could sit by a window and put my bag and typewriter case on the floor beside me. I bought the new *Dime Detective* at the Springfield depot, to give me a little break from reading about the Ozarks. (There's a Rambler Murphy yarn in the *Dime*, incidentally – did I ever tell you he reminds me a little bit of you?)

I'll tell the world I was pretty tired of the trip by the time we began the long downhill run into Mackaville. The tracks curved south-east down a long grade, giving me the opportunity to see the whole town, nestled down in a valley – and I'll be damned if it didn't look like a typical *New England*-style village, laid out around a downtown square, looking neat but out of place here in the South. Maybe Mackaville's founder was from back East. That might explain it. Have to check up on that.

Ahead of the train, I could see what appeared to be a little Hooverville shack-town, just on the outskirts, like they generally are. *Peculiar little shacks*, I thought, straining my eyes in the thickening twilight. I saw movement there in the shadows, but as we drew closer I found that what I thought were humans were *cats* – and they were moving through a grave yard, not a Hooverville. The hovels I thought I saw were actually crypts, and what I took for pieces of junk were crowded, odd-sized tomb stones.

As we rattled by, I watched three of the

biggest cats stop, sit down, and peer silently at the train. They reminded me of the three wise monkeys, and I had a weird fleeting thought about what evil they saw and heard but did <u>not</u> speak of, out there in that cemetery. Just as that notion flew through my brain, one of the cats – a big old calico – hoisted herself up and took a couple of steps toward the train, craning her neck a little, like she was trying to see better. And I swear, John, I could feel her look right straight at me.

You remember Jenny Sorenson telling us how all calicos were female? Her words from all those years ago flashed into my mind then because that damn cemetery cat was staring just like a woman would. Hard to explain, but that's what my seventh sense told me, and we both know enough by now to trust it. Not that I knew what the hell it meant. Just an impression. Still…

Anyhow, I watched her until she and the grave yard were behind us and swallowed up in the gathering dark, with the light from the depot coming into view. I was still dealing with a strong but unfocused premonition, which is probably why I didn't reach down and steady my baggage as the train began to buck with the hard hissing of the brakes. There was a teeth-rattling jolt, and my stuff bounced backward and hit something with a dull thud.

"Dayum!" came an oath from the seat behind me. Then, all of a sudden, like the giant popping up in "Jack and the Beanstalk," a big old blond hill-billy boy in overalls and a dirty undershirt stuck his head over the top of my seat.

"Tayke it easy, yuh pinhead!" he growled.

"Sorry," I said.

I'd had no idea anyone was sitting behind me. The seat had been empty at Springfield, when I'd gotten on the mixed local. He must've boarded at one of the more recent stops.

I bent down and reached back under the seat, figuring the typewriter case had bounced against his foot. I grabbed my bag, but I couldn't locate the case.

"Lookin' fer this?"

I glanced up and saw double. Two hulking straw-haired yahoos that looked exactly alike, right down to the same blank expressions and pale blue eyes. They even seemed to have the same number of bad teeth.

One of them held up my typewriter case and grinned dully. I reached for it, but he pulled it back.

"Reckon this oughta bring some good money," he said to his twin, leering like a big dope, looking at me out of the corner of his eye.

I didn't say anything right away. The train had finally lurched to a stop, and they filed out and headed for the exit. Hoisting my bag, I followed, not letting them out of my sight. That wasn't hard, since there weren't very many people on the train and just a few getting off.

I didn't have much of a plan for getting my typewriter back from those two knuckle- dragging oafs, but I damn sure wasn't going to let them take it, either. So I followed them up the few steps from the track to the platform outside the depot. There were a few people loitering around, and I could feel their eyes on me. Maybe it was the CCC uniform and newsboy cap I wore, or maybe it was because strangers didn't get off the train at Mackaville very often. Either way, I didn't have time to worry about it right then.

The twin with my typewriter case was swinging it like a lunch pail, kind of exaggerated, like his idea of a kid walking to school. As I stepped up next to him, he turned, a big stupid grin on his face.

I sat my bag down, doubled up my fist, and hit him as hard as I could square on the bridge of his nose.

He yelped like a stuck hog and staggered backward a couple of steps, dropping the case. I landed three quick ones, left-right-left, into his midsection, and then caught him with a roundhouse I brought up from around my shoelaces. He stumbled, grabbing at his face, and I snatched up my typewriter case, hoping that his other half would be so dumbfounded by the quick action that I could make a getaway. You know I can box a little bit, but he had at least a foot and fifty pounds on me. Multiply that by two, and I was the kind of long shot even a Damon Runyon character wouldn't touch.

I almost got away. But the other big hillbilly roused himself enough to grab me from behind and sling me to the wood floor of the platform. I managed to hold onto the case with both hands as I went down, hitting with my shoulders and back, but I could see I was going to need those hands pretty quickly. The first guy – crimson dripping between the fingers of the hand he held over his nose – had recovered and was advancing on me, his eyes blazing with rage and pain. The other one drew back and kicked me hard in the side, shooting fiery pinwheels through my whole body.

No, it didn't look good for Robert.

Just as I was bracing for the jar of another boot in my side, I heard a gunshot. Glancing up, I saw the two giant dullards stopped dead in their tracks, looking toward the source of the shot. It was a lawman, badge pinned to his khaki shirt, pointing the barrel of what looked to be an old Remington .44 toward the sky. As I watched, he holstered the revolver and glared at the two, who looked sullenly back.

"He started it, sheriff," muttered the one who'd taken my typewriter, his voice muffled by the bloody hand over his nose.

"He don't look that stupid," returned the sheriff, eyeing me.

"Just a misunderstanding," I said, getting to my feet and hoisting up the typewriter case.

To my left, down on the tracks, there were blasts of steam and lantern lights and whistles signaling that the train was backing into the siding with its freight cars. Then I noticed the half- dozen or so people dotted across the landing, all silent, watching us.

"He *is* that stupid," said the other. "Seth wasn't doin' nuthin' and he jus' come up and *hit* 'im."

"That true, son?" asked the sheriff. He used "son" loosely; although he was a little grizzled, I'll bet he wasn't 10 years older than me.

"Like I said, a misunderstanding. They misunderstood who owned this typewriter." Suddenly out of the darkness hobbled a withered old guy with a full white bristly beard, as rough-looking as Cobb's old horse, who nonetheless gave an impression of power — an impression, I'll add, that was strengthened when he reached up and slapped the hulk called Seth across the back of the neck. Twice the old man's size, Seth still shrank from the blow, pulling his head into his thick neck like a turtle.

"*Git* over here," hissed the old man, not even looking at the sheriff. He reached up and slapped Seth again. Dutifully, the other hillbilly fell in behind the old man and the three walked away, a queer parade. I reached down for my cap, beat it against my thigh a couple of times, and put it back on. The sheriff watched without saying a word, just like the others on the platform.

The only movement was from the two blond behemoths, moving toward the depot and their wizened keeper, still whacking at the injured one with the back of his hand.

I headed back toward the steps to get my

bag, nodding at the sheriff. "Thanks," I said, hoping that would be it. I was ready to call it a night.

"Just a minute."

I stopped and turned. "Yeah?"

"You CCC?"

"Was. Now I'm with the WPA. Folklore project."

He looked me up and down. "How come you're still wearin' your CCC outfit?"

"Hadn't had a chance to get any new clothes yet," I returned. Substitute "money" for "a chance" and it would've been the truth.

"That cap ain't regulation."

"Nope."

"Where'd you get it?"

I measured my words carefully. "CCC, too," I said. "It belonged to a guy who thought he was the toughest man in camp."

"All right," he said, a ghost of a smile playing across his lips. "But we don't need no more troublemakers in town."

I looked toward the depot, where the three had just disappeared through the door. "No," I said. "I don't imagine you do."

After I'd told him my name, and he'd told me he was Sheriff Meagan, we shook hands, parted company, and I walked past the still-gawking locals into the depot. I got directions from the ticket desk to my boarding house and walked outside, passing what I guessed was the town's only taxi, a 1929 Hupmobile with a colored fella dozing at the wheel. I'd been told it was an eight-block walk to Ma Stean's boarding house, and I was tempted, but I thought it best to save the quarter and hoof it. I'd been sitting long enough anyway.

Then a harsh voice cut through the night and my thoughts.

"Hey peckerhead! Better be real careful where yuh step!"

I turned. In the vague light of the depot, I made out the shapes of Seth, his twin, and the old man. I figured it was Seth's brother doing the yelling. It might be too painful for Seth. At least, I hoped so.

"Watch your feet, yuh little bastard!" he added.

The thwack of flesh on flesh ended his soliloquy, and I walked on, wondering what exactly he'd meant. The street lights were on now, the stores were open, and as I made my way down one side of the town square I encountered a good amount of Saturday night traffic. I have to say Mackaville looked a lot more prosperous than I'd figured it would be. I mean, it wasn't downtown Minneapolis, and there were lots of men in overalls and funny hats and women in long dresses and bonnets, but it seemed lively enough. Again, my khaki uniform with its riding breeches and leather leggings got me some stares and funny looks, so I was glad enough to leave the business district behind for the more dimly lit neighborhoods.

Once away from downtown – which was all of three blocks – it was quiet and spooky. But there was a difference. Remember when we were kids back in Hallock, and we'd camp out on our backyards or, later on, out by the Two River? When we were quiet and there wasn't any wind, we'd always hear dogs, barking or yelping or howling in the distance.

It took me a little while to realize I didn't hear any dogs in Mackaville. None. And it was quiet and airless, too, so calm that a fleshy burning odor I'd first caught from the train had really settled in. I knew what it was from my days working in South St. Paul around the stockyards – hard to mistake the smell of a packing house.

Anyway, just as I was thinking how strange it was not to hear any dogs, I suddenly saw a big cat, right in front of me. I swear, John, it was that calico who'd stepped out and locked eyes with me as the train passed by the bone orchard. She stood there for a few seconds and then turned and started walking the same way I was going, her tail standing straight up. Like she was my damn escort or something.

I got the feeling there were other cats out there in the darkness, too, moving as I moved, and the seventh sense started going off in my brain again, even though I didn't know why. All I knew was that this cat, for some reason, triggered it.

I followed her up a hill, and then I saw "Stean" lettered on a mailbox, outside a picket fence. I opened the gate and went up to a big, old-fashioned, Victorian-style house, complete with bay windows and funny little dormers sticking out from the roof. An NRA eagle was affixed to a corner of one of the first-floor windows. It was open, and I heard music – Lanny Ross on Your Hit Parade singing "Jeepers Creepers." It was a welcome sound, and the light from the house was welcome, too.

I looked back as I opened the gate. The old cat eased down on her haunches and watched me as I walked up to the door and knocked. I was still looking back at her when I heard, "You must be Robert! Come in, come in."

I turned to see an ample, dark-complexioned older woman wearing an apron over her dress, her white hair twisted into a bun. And then, the sound of a yippy little rat terrier, running out from behind her to sniff at my boots.

"I'm Ma Stean," she said, sticking out a big hand. I shook it.

"Pleased to make your acquaintance," she continued. "Just drop your bags here for now and come into the livin' room. I want you to meet the others."

Gesturing at the little dog, who looked like an oversized dirty pipe cleaner, she said, "This here's MacWhirtle. We just call him Mac. Old dog. Hope he don't bother you none."

"No. I love dogs." Glancing back, I saw the big cat had disappeared. "He's the first one I've seen since I got off the train."

I saw Ma Stean's gaze follow mine, and I could swear she gave a little nod of her head –

not to the dog or me, but to something or someone else. Odd as it seems, my seventh sense told me it was my now-vanished furry escort.

"Well," she said, still looking out into the night, "this here's kindly a <u>cat</u> town." She turned then, smiling at me. "I saved some supper for you."

Well, John, I felt right then like I was home.

I am typing this in my room on the second floor, which is small but nice, with one of those dormer windows over my bed. I have a roll-top desk for my typing and other work, a lamp, one chair, a rag rug (crazy-colored), a high brass bed, and the bathroom is just down the hall.

That bed is looking good, so 'til next time.

Your pal and faithful comrade,

Robert

May 7, 1939, Sunday evening

Dear John,

I read in a book once that nothing was as bleak as a boarding house room. Not true. Right now, as I sit here writing you, the sunlight's coming through my south window and there's a little breeze, so I don't smell the slaughter-house hardly at all. It's very pleasant. It doesn't quite feel like home yet, but it's a long way from bleak. In fact, compared to the camps, it is pretty luxurious.

Lots has happened since I got in Saturday night and met Ma Stean and her other roomers. When she brought me into the parlor, they were all sitting around the radio, eyeing me as I came in but trying not to be too obvious about it. Ma Stean introduced us, and I shook hands with all three – or, I should say, two hands and a fish flipper. The first one I met was named Dave, a short, very skinny little bald guy with bad front teeth and a goofy grin. He'd been reading an Edgar Wallace mystery and that struck me as a good sign. He was by far the friendliest of the three. Almost before I'd let go of his mitt he'd told me he was single, in town 'til December, and worked as a brass pounder, a telegrapher, at the depot. I also tumbled onto his need for a pal, and that was ok by me. I could use one.

As it turned out, all three of them were rails. Paul, my second introduction, was so tall he made the ceiling look low, maybe six-four or six-five, and not much heavier than Dave. His head was two sizes too big for that pole body and he had a thatch of straw-colored hair that stuck up like it was trying to get away from his head. He wore wire-rimmed glasses with lenses thick as cookies.

Then there was Mr. Clark. Yeah, Mister by-God Clark, no first name volunteered. He was foreman at the railroad repair shop – a stocky, red-faced, balding, heavy-built guy who was all muscle and gristle. He looked like one of those self-important blow-hards who enjoy screaming at people, which made his limp handshake a surprise. Maybe he just gives with the dead fish to avoid crushing the other guy's hand. He's strong enough to do it. Howsomever, it didn't take me long to find out he's a New Dealer all the way, because he approved of my CCC duds and the WPA project that brought me to town. "Hell of a man, that FDR," he said, and offered me a two-bit cigar, which I gladly took, from one fellow traveler to another, if you get my drift.

That catches you up on my first night. I came right to this room, wrote you, and drifted off into the arms of Morpheus, getting up, as usual, in time to watch the sun rise. As soon as I was awake I hopped out of bed and got to the bathroom down the hall, shaved, and took a fast spit-bath in a couple of inches of hot water in that claw-foot tub. I didn't yet know these folks well enough to understand their particular ideas about boarding-house etiquette, so I was fast in and fast out. As a result, I had plenty of time to set my room up, go over my six changes of clothes, mostly CCC, and still be first at the breakfast table when Ma Stean rang the bell at 6:30 a.m. The food was jake – sausage and hotcakes and syrup, fried eggs, milk and coffee – and there was plenty of it.

I didn't learn anything new about the other boarders that morning. Dave was already gone for an early trick on the key, and the other two were trying to zip out to their own jobs and not much for conversation. I guess weekends don't mean much to railroaders. So pretty soon I was left at the dinner table by myself, tacklin' my second stack of wheatcakes, my new chum MacWhirtle looking up at me and maybe hoping I'd slip him part of a sausage. I'd just done that when Ma Stean came in and settled herself where Dave had been sitting, asking me if I was getting enough to eat and shooing the little hound away from the table. That's when I started getting the lay of the land.

First off, I told her about the two big oafs who'd tried to snatch my typer, and the little geezer who'd knocked them around. She told me they were Seth and Sam Black, the twin sons of that whiskery guy. She called him Old Man Black and said I ought to stay away from all three, but especially the dad.

"He's a snake," she said seriously. "A real snake. I ain't kidding. Them boys come from about his fourth or fifth wife. Their mama's dead now, like all the rest of the women who married 'im. You wouldn't think it to look at the old fool, but Ol' Man Black just wears the life right out of 'em, one at a time."

I said I wondered if he was on the list the WPA had sent me, because they'd been keen to find the oldest folks around Mackaville for me to interview, and Black sure looked like he belonged in that group. She said she didn't know, but she'd like to see that list, so I excused myself and went up to my room and retrieved the file, all three sheets worth.

When I brought it back, she cleared off a place on the table and smoothed out the papers, putting on a pair of black-rimmed spectacles and squinting at the names.

"You can see they're mostly on rural routes, and I haven't got very many phone numbers."

"Naw," she said, still studying the list. "Not many phones, 'specially outside of town."

"They're all supposed to have gotten letters from the government telling them I was coming and asking for their cooperation. And I've got a letter of introduction, all official, telling them who I am."

"Uh-huh. That'll be good and well for the ones that can read." She pulled a stubby pencil from the pocket of her apron and started scratching on the paper, pausing between each broad pencil stroke. "Hope you don't mind if I save you a little time."

I got up and peered over her broad shoulder.

About every third or fourth name on the top sheet had a mark through it, and as I watched, she flipped the page and continued working.

"These folks I'm crossin' out," she said, without looking up, "ain't going to talk to you. Ain't nothin' personal, but a lot of people around here don't cotton to strangers, some less than others. You can try 'em if you want to, but you're a-gonna be wastin' your energy."

I watched without saying anything as she lined through several more of the names on my official government document. When she got to the end of the last page, she checked everything over, pushed it aside, and stood up, addressing me in a businesslike fashion.

"Now, since you can't call most of these folks up on the telephone and let 'em know you're comin', here's what you do when you get jest outside their place. Stand there like this and holler." She cupped her hands and shouted, "HALLOOO THE HOUSE!" MacWhirtle, who'd settled himself on a braided rug by the parlor sofa, jumped up like he'd been electrified.

She nodded. "You do that 'case there's any moonshinin' goin' on. A few on your list there been known to brew up a little mash now and again, and they're jus' naturally juberous about strangers sneakin' up on 'em. So you need to announce your arrival. Then when they come out, you tell 'em quick you're with the WPA. Most folks around here knows what that means.

They also know it means you ain't a revenoouer."

"Make sense," I said. "Thanks. What about running into dogs?"

"Ain't many around," she said. "Like I told you, this here's a cat town, and same goes for the hill folks, mostly."

"MacWhirtle seems to do all right." I nodded at the little gray-and-white terrier, who was still on his feet, watching Ma suspiciously after her sudden outburst.

"I've kinda taught him how to get along," she said. "Knew he'd better."

I wasn't quite sure what she meant, but I was beginning to get little glimmers of that old seventh sense again. Then, it all came to me at once: I knew that there was something strange going on in this burg. And I knew it had something to do with the town's feline population. I felt that whatever it was went deep, and I had one of those little shivery feelings skitter through my body. Like, as Grandma Shultz used to say, a crow had just walked over my grave.

I wanted to say something to Ma Stean about the cats, but I didn't know what I could tell her without it sounding like a line from a Lights Out radio show. You've known about my seventh sense for so long – hell, you came up with the name for it – that it's easy to forget most other people would think I was nuts if I mentioned it. I thought maybe I could tell her about the cats I'd seen at the grave yard and the big one I thought was following me to her house, but before I could figure out the right way to approach that with her she started talking about church, and how I was welcome to go with her that morning. I begged off and told her I thought I'd walk around the town a little and see the place in the daylight, kind of get oriented before I started going out and doing my interviews. I thanked her again and left, MacWhirtle following me out the door. Once I got to the gate, though, he stopped, settled onto his haunches, and watched me leave. Before I'd gotten 50 feet away I spied him trotting back to the front door of the boarding house.

I got the odd notion that he might have some...trepidation about the cats in town, and wasn't that a turnaround from the normal way of things?

My fellow roomers may have had to get out early and toil at their rail jobs, but it didn't take long for me to see that blue laws were the rule in Mackaville. The downtown square that had been so busy the night before was all but deserted, except for the people, cars, and a few horse-drawn wagons gathered around the Baptist church just off Main Street. Not even the drug store was open.

I stood in a corner of the square and watched the people arriving at the church for a while, visiting with one another in groups on the grounds, and then the big bell atop the steeple rang, and they all went in. I walked by, and the muffled hymn I heard from inside –

I think it was “Are You Washed in the Blood” – made me feel kind of lonesome. I thought for a minute about going in and sitting down in the back, but instead I walked on, kind of aimlessly, until I realized I’d been unconsciously heading toward the railroad depot. I went by the landing where I’d encountered Moe, Larry, and Curly Black less than a day before, mostly deserted now, and then I kept on going. I didn’t know why, exactly, but that didn’t matter.

Guess where I ended up? The bone yard, that’s where. If I’d seen it in daylight for the first time, I wouldn’t have mistaken it for a Hooverville, even for a minute. But the funny thing was that it gave me the same feeling it had given me when I’d first glimpsed it, as I came in on the train.

This town is weird. And now I know, for sure and certain, it has something to do with cats – all the cats that still prowled around that cemetery in the morning light, and especially that big old calico who peered at me brazenly from behind a chipped and broken headstone.

Your pal and faithful comrade,

Robert

May 8, 1939, Monday night

Dear John,

I don't mean to flood you with letters, but once all this interviewing gets started I may not have a lot of time to write much of anything else. So here's the story of my first work day, sort of, in Mackaville, Arkansas, U.S.A.

Being the new guy in town and not having to punch a clock, I got put on the last bathroom shift, anytime after 6:15 a.m. The good news is I'm not restricted to fifteen minutes like the other three boarders. Since they've all been run through by then, I can stay as long as I want. So I took a real good soak in that old tub and got out just as Ma rang the bell for breakfast.

There was a new addition to the group when I got to the table — and brother, what an improvement. Her name is Patricia Davis. She's 18, in her final year of high school, and she helps Ma Stean during the week before and after her classes. Take the Hedy Lamarr character out of _Algiers_ and transplant her to Arkansas, make her kind of a quiet and innocent but sultry teen-ager, and you'd be close to this Patricia. I am not kidding. Dark, big eyes, swell figure, and before you say anything about cradle-snatching remember I'm only about five years her senior.

Not that I've asked her on a date or

anything. But she sure got my attention, and I was able to chat her up a little bit without sounding like I was on the make. At least I hope so. I was glad I'd taken an extra-long bath and gotten myself presentable.

Meeting her was a bright spot in the day, but that's not saying much, because the rest of it turned out to be pretty crummy. I spent most of the morning and afternoon searching for a car to use in my work, and all I found was that I was a world-class sap to have thought I could find wheels in this burg. I walked every beat-up sidewalk in Mackaville chasing the idea, but chasing was all I did. The town has one dealership, Studebaker, with a total of four heaps sitting on the yard, all of them less than five years old and way out of my price range. What the hell, I gave it a try. The salesman was this thin nasty bastard in a cheap, light blue pin-stripe suit, a once-white shirt and a wide, flaming red tie that I figured he was wearing to keep people from running over him. He looked at me like I was really interrupting his day. He had one of those rodent faces, like a rat or a squirrel, and he stuck a finger about halfway up his nose when he thought I wasn't looking. Geez. I washed my hands as soon as I could after I'd gotten away from there.

The filling station I stopped into had an old roadster sitting out in front with a "For Sale" sign under the windshield wiper. The guy there told me he wanted a hundred bucks for that flivver, and he didn't seem to care whether I was interested or not. I figure my CCC garb – even though they might have recognized it as an officer's uniform – told both him and rat-face that I wasn't a Rockefeller and probably didn't have enough nickels to throw around to make me worth their attention.

By four o'clock I'd crisscrossed the hot red brick streets of Mackaville at least three times and walked out into neighborhoods to check on two ads in the local weekly I'd picked up at the boarding house. I was finding no joy in Mackaville. No. 1, the cars were all too high, and No. 2, the people all acted like I was from the Bureau of Internal Revenue. At one point I started getting mad for no real good reason, telling myself that they would all be laughing or smirking at me if I hadn't been tall, tough-looking, and in a strange uniform. Their accents started grating on my nerves. Even the hue of their skin seemed foreign to me – most of them were a lot darker than the Norwegians and Swedes we're used to back home. Can't quite put my finger on their heritage.

They're coffee-and-cream-colored like some Indians and Mexicans I've seen, but they don't quite fit either of those categories.

Anyway, I don't know if I was angry because I had gotten what I thought was the bum's rush from the salesman and the gas-station guy, or if I was just feeling alone and strange, surrounded by all these different-looking people yammering to each other in their weird accents. I didn't know what was up with me, but I thought I'd better get off the streets before I smacked somebody just for staring at me.

I was hungry, and Ma doesn't serve lunch at the boarding house except on weekends, so on the way back I stopped beside a railroad-car diner on the edge of town – the Busy Bee Cafe. I ordered three hamburgers and a malted, kidded with the little bottle-blonde jane behind the counter, got a forced smile for my trouble, and gave it up. Dropping sixty cents on the counter, I walked on back to the boarding house to eat at Ma's table, her place being the closest thing I had to home.

MacWhirtle seemed happy to see me, and that made me feel a little better. I plopped down at the table and Ma, who was bustling around in the kitchen, brought me out a plate and a clean napkin and told me that Mac had never taken to any of her other boarders like he'd taken to me.

"It wasn't just that piece of my good sausage you fed him this mornin', neither," she said, smiling.

I shrugged and smiled back. "I throw myself on the mercy of the court," I said. Suddenly, I felt pretty good. Funny how some little exchange like that can boost a guy's mood.

You know I've always liked dogs, and most of them like me back. MacWhirtle sure seemed to.

"Okay if I feed him some of my lunch?" I asked.

She shook her head. "I guess," she said,

still smiling. "He'll be beggin' food from you ever' time you sit down at the table."

"Aw, that's ok," I told her, cutting up one of the burgers into little pie slices and feeding him the whole thing, pickles, onions, and all. He loved it. Ma just shook her head.

While I was feeding him, she asked me how my day had gone. I told her, leaving out the way I'd come to feel about her fellow townspeople.

"Hmmm," she said. Then, "Maybe I know a fellah who can help." She told me then that she had a friend who ran the town's Skelly station. I remembered going by there, but I didn't go in, because I didn't see any cars for sale or rent. Plus, I wasn't in the mood to be given the brush again.

But Ma made the call, and when she hung up, she turned to me and said, "Go on over. His name's Pete, and he'll treat you decent."

Funny, isn't it, about how the world can kick you in the nuts, knock you down on your back, but then you get a full stomach and even a hint of hope and you're ready to go again. I almost ran the seven blocks to the guy's place of business.

It sat at the southwest corner of the town square and was, by far, the neatest-looking of the town's three stations — something I'd noticed earlier. The front drive was busy, with three cars at the pumps and a couple more waiting. The guy tending them all was in an officer's peaked hat and one of those blue gabardine uniforms. When he turned toward me for a moment I could see the Skelly patch on his shoulder and the name "Pete" embroidered above the front left pocket of his shirt. He washed windows, pumped gas, and swept out floorboards, all in a kind of blur. I watched him for a minute from across the street, and by the time I arrived at the station he was putting air in the back tires of some old guy's Hudson coupe. He waved me toward the building from where he squatted.

"Go on inside," he shouted over the noise of a couple of rumbling exhausts. "I'll be with you in a minute."

I nodded and walked into the place. Like most filling stations, the inside was small.

Unlike a lot of them, it was immaculately clean, with a shiny yellow-and-black Congoleum floor you could've eaten off of. There was a Coke box by the door, a Captain Midnight bicycle tire and tube rack next to it, and a glass case full of smokes and candy with a brass cash register sitting on top. Not an inch of the place was wasted.

I looked through the window. His business wasn't thinning out any; as quickly as one car left the pump, another took its place. Figuring I'd be there a while, I pulled a Coke out of the ice and water, dropped a nickel on the counter next to his register, and sat down on the Coke box, watching him work.

You look around just as much in a small place as you do in a big one, and I could see through the side door into the grease-pit bay and beyond that through another door into an area I figured for the repair bay. A couple of flats leaned against the jamb of that second doorway. I considered things for a minute and then I walked across that bright yellow floor, which crinkled like cellophane, and through the grease bay to the deflated tires. Just inside the door was the breaker for flats.

Looking out the door, I could see he was still busy as hell. So I took the initiative and grabbed the first tire, flipped it over, and broke it down, checking inside the case for a nail or piece of wire. There wasn't anything, so I took the tube over to a tub of soapy water and shot a little air into it. It didn't take me long to find the hole, and not all that much longer – maybe eight or ten minutes – to patch it and put it back together. I aired it up, bounced it a time or two, and rolled it off to the side, thinking about how many times I'd done something like that during those two summers I'd worked at Ole Andersson's Ashland station.

The guy named Pete came in while I was putting the second tire together, but he only had time to grin at me before another car honked and away he went. I finished up and washed my hands. There wasn't a bit of dirt on me. My CCC officer training, I guess – they caution you about not getting dirty, so that the men will respect you more or some such shit. Keeping myself cleaned up was second nature to me anyway.

I'd tucked my shirt back in and was sitting on the box finishing my Coke when the day's rush seemed to subside all at once. He stepped through the door, let out an exaggerated "whoosh," grinned at me again and stuck out his hand.

That's how I met Pete Barlow.

He was regular-sized, maybe five foot ten, tight build, and a dark complexion like a lot of the other people I've seen in this town. His black hair was close-cropped, and he had very dark eyes that looked right at you, maybe even through you. He had a beak of a nose that gave him kind of an Arab look. You remember my Uncle Chuck, from Lebanon? Pete looks like that.

He had the confident air of the successful small-town businessman, and his handshake was strong and hard.

"How about another Coke?" he asked, nodding at the empty bottle I'd left on the counter.

"Sure. You bet."

He picked up my nickel, beside the bottle. "Here," he said, flipping it to me. "Thanks for the help."

"Glad to do it. You were swamped."

He nodded his head. "Yeah. It was my rush hour. Everybody waiting until after work to gas up for the next day. I get a lot of one-gallon sales." Pulling two Cokes from the box, he handed one to me. "That's a CCC uniform, ain't it?"

"Yeah. Thanks." I took a pull from the wet, ice-cold bottle.

"I don't know of any camps around here."

"Me neither," I said. "And I'm not CCC anymore. I'm doing interviews with old people around Mackaville, in town and back in the hills, for the WPA Folkfore Project."

"Which is why you need wheels," he said. Upending his Coke, he gulped about half the bottle, his Adam's apple bobbing. "Miz Stean told me."

"That's right. I figured I could pick up some kind of old car here in town. I know enough to keep one running. But hell, no one wanted to give me the time of day."

"Yeah," he said, wiping the back of his hand across his mouth. "It's a hard row for any newcomer in this place. They'll thaw out, but it takes a while and you can't wait. You need something to drive and right now."

I nodded. "That's the size of it."

Pointing with the now nearly empty bottle, he indicated a Model T sitting just outside the station. The door of the turtle hull had been removed and a big box sat in its place, fitted snugly down into the trunk.

"I could let you use the shop car for a buck a day, but you couldn't have it until after lunch, and you'd have to have it back by six," he said.

I shook my head. "Naw. I don't know when these people are going to be able – or willing – to talk to me, and if I gave you a dollar a day I'd likely run out of dough before I got my first government check."

"Miz Stean told me she didn't think you had much money."

"Miz Stean ain't lying," I said.

He glanced toward the repair bay – at the two tires I'd fixed, maybe – and seemed to ponder something for a moment.

"I got an idea," he said after a moment. "C'm'on."

I followed him through the grease bay to the other garage. "You know how to ride a motorbike?"

"Sure," I said, lying like I was on a blind date. You could put my knowledge of motorcycles in your eye and not feel a thing. But I remembered the name of the big bike that rich kid Lawrence Morgan used to ride and brag about – remember? – so I added, "I used to run around on an old Excelsior."

The sun was going down now, the front of the station in shadow. "Excelsior?" he said, suddenly bursting into laughter. "That ain't a motorcycle." He flicked on the lights in the bay and walked to the back of the shop, pulling the tarp off the biggest bike in the world.

"<u>This</u>," he announced, "is a motorcycle – a four-banger Indian with a side car."

John, the damn thing was as big as a combine, even without the side car – which had its own windshield. The engine, which sat in some kind of pan arrangement, was twice the size of anything I'd ever seen. I gasped like someone had just thrown a glass of water in my face. I couldn't help it.

Pete Barlow still grinned, but there was something besides humor in the piercing stare of those dark eyes. I could see doubt stirring behind them, and I couldn't have that.

"Hell, I can ride that big monster if you'll give me a lesson," I said, with what I hoped sounded like confidence instead of me whistling past a grave yard. "I know how to fly, I can run a dump truck, I can drive every model Cat made and work a steam shovel, too. This Indian ought to be my meat."

He took my words in without saying anything back, and when he stooped and spent a minute or so rubbing a nonexistent spot off the red polish of the sidecar with a rag from his hip pocket, I knew Pete Barlow was a man who didn't make quick decisions.

Finally, he stood up and faced me. "Tell you what I'd do, if you're interested," he said. "I'd rent you the bike for five bucks a month, cash on the barrelhead, and you come in after your supper for let's say an hour every day and give me a hand closing up. Fix any flats I haven't gotten to. Maybe do some grease jobs. Help me deliver cars. Once folks get used to you, maybe you can help on the drive, too. It'd be every day but Sunday. I don't open on Sundays."

He let me think it over. I'd be working cheap, but the bike would be a lifeline. In fact, I didn't know how the hell I'd be able to do the folklore job without some way to get around to the people I needed to see.

"I may have a late interview every once in a while," I said. "Would you work with me on that? I'd put in extra hours to make up for it."

He nodded, and before he had time to say anything I stuck out my hand, saying, "All right. You've got yourself a new hired man. Show me what to do and I'll start now."

"All right, then." He grinned like a guy picking up his winnings at a crap game. You can't beat a deal that makes both sides happy.

I worked with him through dinnertime that evening. He showed me where things were, and he seemed pleased when he found out I knew all the basics of being a pump jockey. After he'd closed up, he gave me my driving lesson on the big Indian, and I found out why it had been sitting there under a tarp for a while. The last bad wreck had done it for him. It had been his second accident in a year, and he'd had to take a month off work and turn the station over to someone named Diffie, who I doped out was a good guy but maybe not the sharpest tack.

So it may not have been a giant act of charity on Pete's part, but it still solved my transportation problem. I also found out it worked different from any motorcycle I'd ever seen, and steering it was like steering a battleship. Still, I got it figured out fairly quickly and felt confident enough to drive it back to the boarding house, where all the occupants – even MacWhirtle – came out to see what was making all the noise. (I found myself wishing that Patricia was there to see me come roaring in.) Ma let me park it in her empty garage, which is actually more of a shed, with garden tools and other stuff stored in it. But it has a good solid Yale lock on it, so I figure it to be plenty secure.

As soon as I got in the house, before I'd even had a chance to thank her for sending me over to Pete's place, Ma came out of the kitchen with a big thick-sliced ham sandwich and a glass of milk for me. I sat down at the table to eat it, MacWhirtle at my feet, and between bites told everyone about how I'd gotten the motor bike.

On balance, it hadn't turned out to be such a bad day after all.

Your pal and faithful comrade,

Robert

May 13, 1939, Saturday morning

Dear John,

Like I expected when I wrote you last, I've been so busy getting up and running with these interviews, along with helping Pete close up his station every night, that I haven't had time to write for several days. So there's lots to tell you.

First of all, thank you for the good long letter. Minnesota seems a million miles away to me now, so I was especially glad to hear from you — and especially proud to hear that you've placed a yarn with *Weird Tales*. Congratulations, pal! Looks like you've won our old bet about who was going to crack the pulps first. I can't remember what I owe you, but I'll be happy to pay it. That idea about a vampire preacher is a pip. It ought to hit their readership smack between the eyes.

I just looked over that last sentence. Guess I'm starting to use the *patois* I've been picking up around here.

That's not all I've picked up around here. Fact is, I'm getting plenty of ideas for *Weird Tales*-type stories myself. I know working the copy desk at the *Dispatch* puts you front row center on some strange happenings, but this burg can hold its own with St. Paul when it comes to the bizarre. It's like a lot of these people are living in an E. Hoffman Price novel.

Not Lovecraft – he's too far out there – but Price or maybe Wellman.

Okay. I'd better quit beating around the bush and get right to the story.

Last night, I had the crap scared out of me.

I was coming in from doing an interview with an old fellow named Izzy Seamore and his wife, Junie. They live in a little whitewashed shack about a mile outside of town. Actually, his wife turned out to be the loquacious one, and she gave me the best story. It's plenty chilling, and if I can make these keys strike hard enough to get through three sheets of paper and two sheets of carbon paper (I keep a copy of all the reports for myself) I'll send you a copy when I finish writing it up.

On the way back to town on the big Indian, I started experiencing one of those dark feelings I used to get that were, a lot of times, precursors to the seventh sense. I chalked it up to the story the old lady had told me, and wait 'til you read it, but darkness kept getting stronger and stronger, even when I shared the story with Pete as we were closing his service station down.

"Them Seamores are pretty good people," was about all I got out of him.

I got back to the boarding house about dark – had to, since the lights on the bike don't work. Pete keeps saying he'll fix them, and then we get busy and it slips his mind and mine, too. I ate dinner with Mister Clark and

Paul. Dave had gone on the swing shift at the rail yard.

(Patricia wasn't there because she only works mornings and weekends – I saw her just an hour or so ago, though, and we're getting pretty chummy. Boy, what a baby!)

There's a twofer rack at the grocery story just down the street, where you can trade two pulps for another or buy the used ones for half-price. I'd gotten four really good ones while I was on my lunch break that day – a Shadow from '35, a Doc Savage from '36, a Weird Tales – your new employer – from all the way back to '29, and a hot damn Spicy Adventure from '35, all four for 30 cents. They were all new to me, in good shape, and I couldn't wait to get to them.

I chose the Doc first, and I finished the whole story by about midnight, another good effort by old Kenneth Robeson that takes Doc and the boys to the South Pole. I was reading in bed, under one of those lights that hooks over your headboard, and while I thought about finishing off with one of the three backup stories in the mag, my eyes were getting heavy. So I switched off the light, and I'll admit I was thinking about Patricia, and I don't mean Doc's cousin, as I drifted off.

I think I told you that my room was on the second floor, with a big window right next to the bed. Well, John, all of a sudden I was wide awake, lying on my side and staring out that window into the moonlight. I lay there confused for a minute, wondering why I'd awakened, and then I heard the sound on the other side of the room, behind my back. Someone was at my desk, going through my papers and being very sneaky about it, trying not to make any noise. Still, I could pick it up plainly enough. Two or three pages would flip, and then I'd hear this little scraping or scratching, like when somebody runs a fingernail down a piece of paper.

I want you to know that as I lay there in the pitch dark, my eyes fixed on the moonlit scene outside, I figured I was a dead duck. What could I do? I kept listening, and every once in a while I thought I heard heavy breathing.

I don't know how long I lay there, not moving a muscle. Maybe it was only a couple of minutes. Because my back was to the rest of the room, I knew that if I rolled over whoever or whatever it was would be on me before I could even jump up. I am here to tell you I felt the kind of terror you and I have only read about, and it was damn near unbearable. I knew I had to do <u>something</u>.

Very slowly, I calmed myself down and took stock. My left hand was resting on the pillow, and I decided that my best course of action was to slowly, <u>very</u> slowly, slide it up the headboard to the reading lamp and flip it on. At the same time, I'd yell at the top of my lungs.

I was frightened nearly out of my mind, and at the same time I was mentally cussing you because your making fun of me was the reason I did not sleep with my pistol under my pillow anymore.

Well, every nerve in my body was screaming from tension as I moved my hand, slowly, silently, up to that light switch. I can't explain how good that little knurled knob felt when my fingers finally touched it. Gathering myself up, I switched it on, whirling around and shouting something like, "YAAAAAAHHHHH!"

The room exploded with light, and something else exploded at my desk. Papers flew into the air, a tumbler half-full of water clattered to the floor, and a big old calico cat shot up the wall, clawed frantically at the door moulding, and bailed out through the transom like her life depended on it – which it did, because I would've killed that son-of-a-bitch if I could've caught her.

I climbed out of bed to retrieve my papers, some of which were already wet from the spilled water, and it wasn't long before there came frantic knocks at my door. I threw on some pants and an undershirt and pulled the door open. Everybody in the house was there, even MacWhirtle, peering in at me like they thought I'd gone mad.

When I told them what had happened, though, they laughed. Thank God they thought it was funny. I had visions of being put out onto the street in this strange little burg with no place to go.

I didn't think it was too damned funny, though. Because in the split second between the light coming on and the cat scaling the wall and shooting through the transom, I saw a couple of things that right now give me goose pimples, even on this bright and sunny morning.

I'd bet money my intruder was the same old cemetery cat that ushered me to this place last Sunday. And, John, I'd bet double that I caught it reading the notes from my interviews.

More later,

Robert

May 14, 1939, Sunday afternoon

Dear John,

I am feeling over my jitters now and sometimes it even seems a little funny, that whole thing about the cat in my room looking over my notes. It's funny in another way, too. Funny odd. Because even though everybody here at Ma Stean's seems amused by my outburst Friday night, I know there's something going on. Remember that essay that Lovecraft wrote about cats, and how they're close to things that people can't see? I've been thinking about that.

And speaking of old H.P.: There's one of his yarns in the Weird Tales I bought at the grocery, but I've put it aside for a while. It's weird enough around here.

Ma asked me to church again this morning, but I turned her down gently and told her I was going to take the morning and explore the countryside. She looked at me a little funny, but not mean or anything, and told me to be careful.

So I got on the big Indian about 7:30 this morning and took off for the hills, winding through a lot of woods and wilderness. Here everything is green and lush, all up and down, hills following hills, row upon row, little valleys with shacks and animal pens and crop rows hidden from each other by ridges and dark bands of trees. Sometimes the evergreens and old hardwoods were so thick and tall that going past them plunged me into a kind of twilight.

I was popping away through one of those stretches, heading back toward town, and I suddenly felt sure that someone on horseback was coming up behind me. When I glanced back I didn't see anyone, but I couldn't shake the feeling so I opened her up and went tearing away down a hill. Hell, I'm not sure now why I even did that, but at the bottom I ran into a dry creek bed that was about a foot deep in pea gravel.

Talk about an explosion! That crap blew out around me like I was a speed boat and it was my wake. I thought I was going to roll the bike for sure, but I shot on across – how I don't know. That stuff is round and loose and slippery and I had a hell of a time staying upright. But I did. I am still shaking those little rocks out of the Indian.

Even though I made it across the gravel, I didn't get off scot-free. Just as I topped the next hill the Indian started missing and then quit dead on me. I had to get off and push her in for the last five miles. Since it was Sunday, Pete wasn't open, so I wrangled her into Ma's garage and went in the house and cleaned up, figuring to get to Pete's station early tomorrow. So now, after a good bath, I'm at the roll-top in my room writing you and wondering about the bike. I figure one of the rocks may have kicked up and busted something up in the engine.

Looking around this room I think it's funny how it's become home already. I've only been here a little over a week and in some ways it's like I've lived my whole life in this burg. The brass bed, the funny little rag rug, even old MacWhirtle, who's right now sitting at my feet – have I really only lived here for a week?

It makes me feel good to write you. The next best thing to talking.

Most of the interviews I've gotten so far have just been standard stories about grandparents and other people from a long, long time ago – I've heard a couple from as far back as the 1700s – and how they lived back then, but Mrs. Seamore, the woman I wrote you about yesterday, gave me a real dandy. I've finished writing it up and I hope that the carbon I'm sending along is dark enough for you to read. I think it is. I gave you the one I usually keep, the first copy, and took the second and lighter one for my own records. It wouldn't surprise me if you found enough in it for another Weird Tales story. In fact, I'm thinking that I'm going to find enough stories around here to keep us both in Weird Tales-type plots for a good long time.

I'm still trying to get the accents right, so you'll see that I'm recreating what I heard phonetically. It may be kind of hard to read. I took it all down in that part-shorthand method we devised when we were kids and wanted to write stuff down that only we understood. That seems to work. Helps that these people talk pretty slowly.

One more thing. Mrs. Seamore, who's from back east and only came here with her husband about 25 years ago – they wanted to go west and got this far before they ran out of geetus and he went to work at the packing plant – seemed really keen on the subject of witches. She said they see everything clearer than we do but pea gravel messes 'em up. They stand and look at it so long that they finally give up and leave. So if whomever I heard or <u>thought</u> I heard following me on horseback up there in the mountains this morning was a witch, I guess that pea gravel I drove across stopped whatever it was dead in its tracks.

You might want to file that away. Never know when a witch might be following you, and not the kind you've gone on dates with.

I'm only half-kidding. Maybe not even half. It could be that the story from Junie Seamore that you're about to read got to me more than I want to let on, but I've been thinking a lot about witches and I wouldn't be surprised at all if this town's got a few. Like I told you at the beginning of this letter, I get an overwhelming feeling that there's something dark and strange in this place. Something big. I think it's the seventh sense sure enough, even though what it's telling me is still pretty vague. Witches and cats have something to do with it, but past that connection everything gets all blurry. I'll dope it out, though. I know I will.

Meanwhile, here goes another six sense — I mean <u>cents</u>. You don't have to airmail me, but be sure and write and tell me what you think about the enclosed account from Mrs. Seamore. It's a hair-raiser.

Your procurer of tall tales,

Robert

WORKS PROGRESS ADMINISTRATION--FEDERAL WRITERS' PROJECT

Official Form

DATE: 12 May 1939

INTERVIEWER: R.A. Brown

STORY TOLD BY: Izzy (Junie S.) Seamore AGE: 74

ADDRESS: Star Route 3, Mackaville, Arkansas

When my Gran'mammy Zula wuz jest a little un, 'bout waist high, she usta go en stay with her Gran'mammy Rachel for a spell to kinda hep thet ole woman and to larn from her. Wunst when she done that they had a spot o' witch trouble. It was lak this...

Li'l Zula wus a'churnin' the cream 'n' she an' her Granny was jest havin' a fine time, a-jawin' and a-laughin'. After while her Gran'-mammy says, "Chile! Ain't thet butter a-comin' yet? Let me see thet." She tooken the churn from Zula, lifted th' top off, and shore nuff it weren't nuffin' but cream.

"Now thet just ain't right!" she said. "It ain't right! Chile, I 'spects we's bein' witched!"

Zula was too young to know eny better 'n' she claps her hands and says, "Granny, will we see the witch? Kin she fly and ebber thing?"

Well, her Gran'mammy grabs her by th' shoulders 'n' slaps her jaws right smart. "Don't you NEBBER speak of a witch lak they was anything 'ceptin' death and sorrow."

Zula was plum skert by how mean her Gran'mammy was actin'. But her Gran'mammy loved thet chile too much to stay angry wiff her. "Less jus' see if'n' we cain't stop thet ole witch's devilment," Gran'mammy Rachel says.

She had Zula take her li'l hands 'n' scoop up some of the cream in the churn. Then they went over to th' fire.

"Here, witch!" sez Gran'mammy Rachel. "Git burnt for yer troubles!" Then she throwed that cream on th' fire.

"NOW we'll get butter, chile," she says. "Jest see if'n we don't." But no matter how hard they churn, they couldn't get no butter.

Zula's gran'mammy then tole her, "Zula, baby, you go out and empty thet lil trough, dump it out." Zula run and did as she'uz tolt. Her gran'mammy come out a'luggin' thet churn and poured thet cream into thet trough. Zula's eyes got ez big ez dollars et thet. Her gran'mammy seen her a'starin' an' tells her, "Chile, we got more cream but thet ole cream coulda kilt us!" Then she pinted down th' valley an' acrost to where they wuz annuder cabin.

"Thet slattern witch Jury Maggan thinks she's smart, but I got this!" She holded up a bit a' rag cloth. Zula wondered at thet cloth en her gran'mammy sez, "I seen her git it teared off'n her dress on them bramble breshes yonder." She pinted to a thorn hedge by th' road. "Now I'm a'gonna give it back to her!"

Gran'mammy Rachel dropped thet rag into thet cream. Then she wen' over to her prize rose-bushes that no one wuz allowed to tetch and cut seven long switches, 'bout big round ez your lil finger en 'bout two foot long. She took thet bundle uh switches and come back to thet trough o'cream and bugn to slash and whop thet cream. She busted thet cream with ebber bit o' her stren'th en cream flew eberr where.

Zula watched thet ole woman, face red ez fury, jest slashin' an' wackin' thet trough – and then she heered it. That li'l chile spun 'round en looked down th' road, 'crost to Jury Maggan's cabin, and heered horr'ble scream after horr'ble scream echoin' down th' valley.

Behind her, her gran'mammy sez, "Zula, baby, less go churn us some butter now."

May 20, 1939, Saturday evening

Dear John,

I am going out of town to the movies in a little bit with Pete from the Skelly station and his friend, Diffie, the guy who ran things for him after he cracked up on the Indian motor bike I'm now driving, so I may have to finish this tomorrow. But I wanted to tell you I got your letter and thanks for the words about the Seamore story I sent you. Like you said, it's a chiller for sure.

I would have gotten back to you sooner but have had my hands full. Hmmm, maybe I should reword that. Truth is I have been a little lazy and it's taken most of my energy to keep the interviews typed and in the mail. I'm learning so much on this job. Sometimes I feel like I'm learning a little <u>too</u> much. I can't shake the feeling that this town has some kind of secret, and it has to do with that cat in my room, and it has to do with the witch story I got from Mrs. Seamore, and it has to do with just the way the people <u>look</u> – as crazy as that sounds. I can't dope it all out yet, but it's there, and <u>you</u>, better than anyone on God's green earth, <u>know</u> how I know.

Speaking about how people look, I got a letter from some damn registrar or comptroller or something at the Arkansas state capitol. This is a WPA project I'm on, and the state governments really don't have anything much to do with it, but somehow this old boy got word about what I was doing and sent me a big official letter telling me he would "appreciate" me sending him the names of anyone I interview that I thought might be, get this, "passing as white." Yeah. "Passing as white." <u>There's</u> a guy in solid with Uncle Adolf. Of course I don't intend to tell him shit, but if I told him what I thought about the background of this town's population, I figure he'd be hightailing it up from Little Rock to see for himself. That creamed-coffee color so many of them have – even Patricia – indicates to me that there's a pretty good amount of Negro blood coursing through the veins of most of the citizens in this town. Why? Hell, it's just another one of the mysteries around here that I wake up thinking about.

After I'd sent off the first few reports, I decided I'd better let the postmaster, a severe- looking guy by the name of Gibson, know why I was mailing so much stuff on a regular basis to Washington. Even though he's middle-aged, he's kind of prune-faced, like a guy a lot older would be. He's got real pale blue eyes, although he's as dark as the others I just mentioned.

Anyway, I saw him behind the window yesterday and told him my name and what I was doing.

He looked at me sort of hostile-like and said, "Yeah, I figured you for a gov'ment case." Case, he said. Whatever the hell that's supposed to mean.

Then he said, "You're writin' about our people?"

"That's right. Getting their stories down for posterity."

He looked at me a long time. Then he said, "Better be careful," and before I could ask him what he meant by that, he turned away from the window and disappeared. I got the distinct impression he didn't approve of my assignment. If I wanted to get melodramatic about it, I could even say I got a little glimmering of the seventh sense.

So that's my life in Mackaville, Arkansas. I think I've hit most of the low spots, and I've sure given you plenty about the weird feeling that always seems to be hanging around me. My fellow federal employee the postmaster aside, I guess I'm doing ok as a cog in the government's efforts to spread money around. I think I told you that Ma Stean's boarding house gets a U.S. treasury check for my room and board. Even though it can't be much, maybe it gives me some prestige with her, because in addition to the morning and evening meals I can always get some kind of snack, a jelly sandwich or cookies, whenever I want it. Or maybe she's just naturally a nice person who looks out for others. I think I'd rather believe that.

Physically, I'm comfortable enough. The summer heat is starting up, but because of the big window, my room stays reasonably cool. And

Ma and the boarders know I'm a "writer" for the federal government and they think that's noteworthy, so they don't kick when I sit up and type late into the night.

Pete finally fixed the headlight on the Indian, so now I can maneuver that big bike around after dark. But I don't do that much yet, and when I do, well, I always feel like someone's following me. I wrote you about that in the last letter, remember? I don't think I told you that every time I look back through the darkness, I swear I can see something or someone behind me, just far enough back that I can't make out what it is. Sometimes I think I hear horse's hooves. I know it's most likely not true. But if it's not, why do I feel it?

I never slow down or anything to make sure it's just a phantom. I don't know what I'd do if it caught up to me anyway. So I just hunch over the handlebars and crack that old Indian open another notch. Those hill people must wonder who it is roaring through their countryside, but if you were on that empty road with me, moonlight spearing down through the trees, some real or imaginary apparition on your heels, you'd be kicking me to go faster.

We're driving to a bigger town tonight to take in Adventures of Robin Hood, which I know has already played in St. Paul. I'll bet you've seen it, too. But I haven't yet and I'll be glad to, although I wish I were going with Patricia instead of two guys. My own fault.

When it comes to romance, I'm just as much of a slow worker in Arkansas as I was back home.

When I do take her out, I'll probably ask her to the nicer of the two theaters in town, which is called the Palace. (The other, the Maribel, shows B-picture double features.) I imagine Robin Hood will eventually get to the Palace as it works its way from the big cities to the little-town picture shows. Maybe by the time it makes it to Mackaville I will have gotten up the nerve to ask Patricia for a date.

Pete already knows I've got a case on her. The other day, while I was helping him at the station, Patricia drove up in this 20-year-old Chevy four-passenger roadster with an old lady sitting up straight as a ramrod in the back. Hot as it was, she was all dressed in black, trimmed with lace that looked like it would crumble if you touched it, and was she some kind of UGLY. I mean she was witch ugly. Of course, if there'd been ten witches in the back seat, I still would've gone over there and waited on Patricia.

It was during the late-afternoon rush, so I didn't get to talk to Patricia much, and I've got to admit that when I was chatting her up I kept sneaking glimpses at that flesh-and-blood phantasm behind her, who stared back at me through half-closed eyes, like a big black lizard. Although I couldn't see them clearly, her pupils seemed to be real light-colored, almost translucent, which just added to her overall look.

After they'd left, I started working on the next car in line. It wasn't until almost closing time that things settled down, and Pete and I stood together at the pumps, looking out at the street.

"That Patricia Davis is a pretty little thing, ain't she?" he said. Taken by surprise, I whirled around to find him grinning at me.

"You bet," was all I could think of to say.

"She's smart, too. Just graduated high school, and I wouldn't be a bit surprised if she went off to college."

"She's graduated?" That surprised me. No one around the boarding house had made a big deal about her graduation. But then I thought, Well, what's the difference? I haven't even asked her out yet. It wouldn't have seemed proper for me to get her a graduation gift.

"Yeah. Night before last. Top of her class."

"She is that," I said softly. Then, "Who was that old harridan with her?"

Pete chuckled. "Why, that's her grandma, Miz Davis," he said.

"What?"

"That's right."

I shook my head. "How can a battle-ax like that have such a beautiful granddaughter?"

"Well, now, you don't know what she looked like when she was a young lady," he said, still smiling. "She might've been every bit as pretty as Patricia."

With that, he strode into the station to start shutting down, leaving me to think about what he'd said. And I have to admit that I did think about it.

Well, I just heard a horn honk outside and looked down from my window to see Pete in his green '36 Hudson. Guess the guy sitting next to him is Diffie.

Write when you can. It's lonesome here in a way.

Robert

May 21, 1939, Sunday afternoon

Dear John,

It's four o'clock p.m. and I've just now started feeling good enough to write you. As a guy who doesn't drink all that much – and the way I feel now, I'm never drinking again – I'm not used to big-time hangovers. I don't see how guys like Steinbeck and Hammett and even Errol Flynn handle the amount of sauce they're supposed to toss down their gullets on a regular basis.

Flynn, by the way, did a hell of a job in Robin Hood, something I'm sure you know already. I didn't find it out for myself until last night, after well over an hour's drive to a place called Harrison, which they tell me is the biggest town around. It was big enough to have an MGM house called the Gem Theatre. (I'm sure that both the picture shows in Mackaville are independents. Today, the Palace is running a Charles Laughton movie called The Beachcomber, while the Maribel has Karloff in one of his Mr. Wongs from Monogram, with a second feature so old it's sprouted chin whiskers.)

I have to tell you about this Gem Theatre. It was a play house to begin with and it had these little boxes or balconies down the side, reached by narrow stairs. We thought about sitting in one of them, but we agreed that we wanted to be closer to all the Technicolor action, so we found a spot about two-thirds down.

The Palace has a giant screen and, man, it was a great movie. I thought Diffie, who's kind of simple, was going to get us kicked out. He'd get excited and start yelling. In case you haven't seen it, there's a scene where someone sticks a spear through the back of Robin's chair. Diffie yelled, "Gawd dayumn!" pretty loud and some lady went and told on us. The usher came down and chewed all three of us out, and we got Diffie calmed down so we wouldn't get the bum's rush.

But it was great. Everything was so huge on that screen. Any time Pete wants to go, I'm in for gas money.

On the way back, we stopped to eat a late dinner at a bar and grill called the Rooting Hen. Man, when I walked in that door and looked around, I thought I'd been set up and I'd never get out. It was an old Negro dive, and "dive" fits. Turns out it was a place built by gangsters back during the dry years, complete with secret panels, trap doors, tunnels, and steel boiler plate in the walls. I know this because they showed me everything.

But like I said, at first I figured I was done for. When I pushed open the door and walked in, ahead of Diffie and Pete, the place went from a loud roar to nothing but the juke box playing. You talk about <u>hostile</u> – until they saw Pete. Then everything was ok and they – "they" being about 100 colored people – all came by to talk to him. He kept saying how I was a famous author and was on their side and was going to write some good things about them.

John, it went from razors to being their bosom pal. I don't know exactly why. Like I've told you, I suspect there's a lot of Negro blood in Mackaville's residents, and maybe the owner is some distant relative of Pete's. For whatever reason, the guy welcomed me and took me through the whole history of the bar. After going with him down through some dripping tunnels that were dark as the pits of hell, we ordered up food and ate. Oh my gosh, ate is a feeble word for what we did. We had fried chicken and bar-b-q ribs and it was the best of either I have ever eaten. We also had greens and sweet potatoes and fried corn dodgers. Plus beer. A lot of beer. I thought I was full two or three times before we got out of there.

While we were eating and drinking and listening to that kind of bawdy race music on the juke, some of the Negroes got to telling me stories, throwing in a lot of colored slang. I knew a few terms already from the camps. You remember before director Fechner separated whites and coloreds into different groups, about four years ago I guess, several CCC camps had guys from both races mingled together. A few of the fellows I served with had been in those camps and picked up the Negro patois. So I knew they called us "ofays" and what dirty terms like "jellyroll" meant. These boys taught me some new ones, though.

At one point in the evening, they started passing around a bottle of whisky. They called it "conk-buster," and it was plenty powerful. Then one of them started telling a story whose main character was a "dusty butt," which I gathered meant a low-class lady of the evening, who got in with a "pancake." When I asked what that was, another fellow told me it referred to a subservient type of Negro man. He actually used the word "subservient." And then, when we dug into that feast, they told me we were "collaring a hot."

I took notes as fast as I could, but I know I missed some of what they were saying. Seems like five or six were talking at once, telling stories, all vying for my attention.

And then, something happened that's been on my mind ever since. One of the men in this Rooting Hen was a small guy with a beard like puffy cotton, sitting at a table with a really big mammy-type. He'd been hitting the brew pretty hard and was slurring his words, but I could tell he wanted to be in the conversation. I was sitting at the bar with Pete and Diffie and a lot of guys, the place full of smoke and music and everyone talking over everyone else, and finally this old gentleman kind of staggered up and leaned in.

"You boys tellin' this ofay writer all kinda stuff," he said, grinning at me. "You gone tell 'im 'bout th' cleansin', that this year be the jub'lee of the cleansin'?"

Well, John, it was like a B-western when the hero pushes through the barroom doors.

Every bit of talk suddenly stopped and all I could hear was a raspy-voiced Negro on the jukebox singing about somebody dusting his broom. All around me, eyes had turned toward the old man, and the eyes weren't slack and friendly anymore. They seemed to be, I don't know, full of <u>warning</u>. Of course, I was full of <u>beer</u>, and a few pulls of whisky, too, but I wasn't so blotto that I didn't know something had changed in that room, and in a damn big hurry.

Whatever it was, the old guy got the message. He staggered back like he'd been shot, muttering out something that sounded like an apology, as the woman at the table pulled him back into his seat by his belt loops, her eyes flashing to our group. Things only stayed like that for a few seconds, but it seemed like forever – that fellow on the jukebox singing about his broom the only sound in the whole joint. Even the smoke seemed to stop swirling and just freeze in place.

I turned to Pete and started to say something, just to hear the sound of someone else's voice. But then one of the patrons passed the whisky – I mean, the conk-buster – to me and said, "Drink up, writer. We gots <u>lots</u> more stories."

Well, I did, and things became a little confused not long afterwards. I remember riding in the back seat of Pete's Hudson and asking him something about what the old man said. It seemed like Pete and Diffie looked at each other funny before Pete told me something dismissive. I can't remember what he said, but I remember it had to do with listening to "old fools."

Although I didn't make a big deal of it, I think – I <u>feel</u> like – there's something more to it than that. Maybe one day Pete will tell me. For right now, though, it's just another piece in the mystery I've somehow stumbled onto.

Cats. Witches. And now, the "jubilee" and the "cleansing." If all those are pieces of a jigsaw puzzle, how many more pieces will I need before I can start seeing the big picture?

We didn't get out of the Rooting Hen 'til after midnight and I have notes for twenty or so different stories, plus another dozen names and addresses. And except for that incident with the old man, none of those people could have been any nicer to me, a white boy from another part of the country. I know a lot of it had to do with Pete and maybe even Diffie, but still…

You know what I'm going to do? I'm going to write every one I've got addresses for and thank 'em for being so nice to me. That's the least I can do.

All this writing and the beer and conk-buster hangover is catching up to me again. Plus, I haven't eaten since that bacchanalian dinner and now I'm starting to get a little hungry. Ma sometimes puts out sandwiches on the weekends. I think I'll go downstairs and see if she's done that yet.

After I eat, I'll see about writing a few of those folks back around Harrison, and then I'm turning in early. So I guess this is all you're getting from me this round. Write back when you can.

Your pal,

Robert

P.S. Pete's a wonderful guy. You gotta meet him.

May 23, 1939, Tuesday morning

Dear John,

I have been doing ok. Had another nutty, no, <u>weird</u> thing happen. Not quite another jigsaw piece. More like the same piece showing up again in the pile.

First let me say that I LOVE Franklin D. Roosevelt! I got a letter today from D.C. telling me that I have qualified for a promotion to clerk-typist GS1 with a salary of $1800 a year.

Wowsers! When I finish here in a few months I will be reassigned to Our Nation's Capitol. The letter didn't say so, but I'm sure they need a lot of us fellows, and gals, in Washington because of the defense build-up. Sooo, the Devil bless Hitler. Without his little toothbrush-moustache craziness I would still be a temporary WPA Field Operative with no prospects after this job is over. My big step up as a public servant hasn't happened yet and I know not to count my chickens, etc., but God bless FDR. I'll be a yellow-dog Democrat forever.

From dog to cat. Yes, that damned calico has been in my room again. I woke up last night just like before, scared to the core by <u>something</u>. This time, when I opened my eyes I was facing my desk and in the moonlight I could see the thing clearly, sitting there, pawing at my papers. The sight froze my spine. I lay there not moving so much as an eyelid for I don't know how long, my heart thudding against my ribs, until that paralyzing feeling of terror began to fade. My eyes adjusted until everything was in sharp focus, and every little movement of that godforsaken animal seemed magnified. I found myself gripped by the fear that she would turn her head and fix her cat eyes on *me*.

I look at those words and try to imagine what you'll think when you read them. But John, I have to tell *someone* this stuff. I can't tell anyone here. They'd think I was a candidate for the laughing academy. I'm afraid you might figure this is some elaborate joke I'm playing on you, trying to get you to fall for something that I'm just making up. I think back to how we both grew up, loving magic and the supernatural and studying it and even trying to see if we could conjure stuff up ourselves – and getting damn close, as you very well know. But this doesn't have anything to do with that. I've also thought that maybe you've got it in your head that I'm doing this to show you I can write a scary yarn just as well as you can, especially after your *Weird Tales* sale. But please don't think any of those things. I swear what I'm telling you is true.

I watched that cat for three or four good minutes, until I was *sure* she was reading my stuff. I thought I could even see the cold moon-glint changing in her eyes as they ran up and down the pages.

Finally, I couldn't take it any more. I yelled, just like I'd done the first time I'd caught it in my room – but this time, instead of taking off, she turned and <u>stared</u> at me. Now that both scared me and pissed me off.

After her first visit, I decided I didn't give a tinker's damn about how you'd razzed me about keeping a gun under my pillow, so I flipped the light on and came out with my .22 revolver. This time I got the reaction I wanted. Those eyes got big as milk saucers and that baby blasted across my desk, skidded on the papers, got tangled up in the chair legs, and went halfway up the wrong wall before getting it right and vaulting out of the transom like before.

Maybe it was a nervous reaction, but seeing that big old cat go from scary to terrified made me burst out laughing. I couldn't help it. The minute before, she had been staring me down like she was the Devil's own, not a bit afraid. And then, when she saw the gun, complete panic and a pratfall under the chair. I laughed and laughed until Ma knocked at my door, having heard me holler, I guess, and undoubtedly wondering just what in hell was wrong with me, although she was nice enough not to say it.

We just finished breakfast, and Ma didn't bring up the subject of my outburst last night. I appreciate that, especially since I don't know what Patricia would've thought, and she was right there serving up the food to me and Paul and Mr. Clark. (Dave's on the early trick again.) If either of them heard me holler last night, they didn't say anything either. So Patricia doesn't have to worry about going out with a crazy man. Not that I've asked her yet. But I'm getting up the nerve.

Trying for several interviews today out in the hills. It's cloudy and at breakfast Mr. Clark said there was a big thunderstorm on the way and maybe a tornado. Apparently it's the season for those. So I'd better rev up the big Indian and get on my way.

More in a day or two.

Your faithful pal,

Robert

May 24, 1939, Wednesday afternoon

Dear John,

No tornado, but we had a lot of thunder and lightning last night, changing to a light but steady rain by daybreak. It rains a lot here, which is why everything is so green. Wet air comes in and hits the Ozarks, rises and cools and dumps buckets of H2O on us. At least it pushes the temperature down several degrees and you don't smell the slaughterhouse at all.

I talked to a couple of neat old people today, going up the highway north about five miles and then west on dirt roads another five or so. If I hadn't had my goggles I wouldn't have been able to make the trip. As it was, I slowed way down when I hit the dirt roads. They were now topped with an inch or two of thin mud, making it tricky, but even slipping and sliding from one side of the road to the other I kept going. When I was done with the second interview, it took me right at an hour to get back on the highway. Man, that old blacktop sure looked good. Even though the rain water was splattering and blurring my goggles, I got back to Ma Stean's in jig time with my papers nearly dry. I took a hot bath right there in the middle of the day, sitting in the tub and talking to MacWhirtle for a good half-hour. Now I feel like a new man and figured I'd write you to warm up the typer before I start working on the stories.

Even though it was an awful long ride through the rain, it was worth it. Both of the yarns I collected were about, you guessed it, witches. One was told to me by a 90-year-old woman, Maria Williams, about an old lady her ancestors found out was a witch. They killed her son, who was feeble-minded, but she got her revenge. The other was a great story about "witched guns" from Boyd Bird Barling of Flat Gap – honest! – who heard the tale from his grandpappy who heard the story from his grandpappy who was there. That puts the action back about 120 years, which is a common period for these stories I'm gathering. Boyd Bird is 78 years old, and he heard the story as a kid 60 years ago from a man who'd heard it as a boy 60 years before that. So the setting is early in the last century, say the 1820s, when this part of the U.S.A. was pretty much a raw wilderness full of wild Indians and lots of other perils. I can understand why it's a great idea to collect these stories. I and others like me with this Folklore Project are opening windows to the past that will soon be shut forever, because I don't think the kids and grandkids of this generation really care. In fact, the few I've run into around here don't even seem to understand why I'm doing what I'm doing.

The old folks, though, they know, and it's important to them. But I have to admit that a lot of 'em don't quite savvy the whole picture. Yesterday, when I was helping Pete shut down, a deeply tanned old fellow wearing new bib overalls over a red union suit faded almost to pink came into the station office and asked, "You thet fella takin' down all our folks' stories, ain'tcha?"

I said I was.

He looked me up and down for a minute without speaking. Finally, he said, "You bein' hurtful?"

"What?" I asked.

"You bein' hurtful in what you writ?"

Pete was back in one of the bays, so he wasn't there to translate for me. The best I could gather, the old boy wanted to know if I was making fun of the people I interviewed.

"Nossir," I said. "I'm being respectful."

He took off his wide-brimmed straw hat and produced a polka-dotted blue handkerchief from his overalls pocket, stirring around the slickness on his browned brow. Then he nodded and stuffed the cloth back inside his front pocket.

"That's good," he said. "All them folks knows you're here, and they wonderin' whatcha up to."

"My intentions are good. I just want to get the old stories on the record before they disappear," I said. "For the government."

He nodded again, but this time I thought I saw the same flash of warning in his eyes that I'd seen from the storytellers back at the Rooting Hen.

"Jus' make sure you tell 'em good, then," he said.

"I will."

He turned to go. Just as he reached the door, he turned around. "And son," he added, "you don't need to tell everythin' you hear."

I opened my mouth to respond, but before I could say anything, he'd shuffled out the door and was heading past the pumps. As I watched him go, Pete came out of the bay, wiping his hands on a rag.

"You know who that is?" I asked, pointing toward the retreating back of the old guy.

Pete squinted. "Yeah." He paused, studying the rag. In the short time I'd known him, I'd come to understand that his silence and pretended attention to something else meant he was carefully deciding what to say next.

"He's a Gabber," Pete said finally. "They're thick as flies in this town and all through the hills. Gabbers own the packin' house and most of the rest of Mackaville. You've prob'ly run into some of 'em already."

"Not yet."

"Well, now that I think about it, you have. Diffie's a Gabber. Barely. He and his old man are shirt-tail relatives of the brothers who own Gabber Meats. Diffie's pop is some kinda pencil- pusher at the plant. Lots of Gabbers on hog farms outside town, too. You got any of 'em on your gummint list?"

I tried to remember. "Seems like maybe I do," I said.

"Just make sure to holler before you try to go in one of their houses to do your interviewin'. Them Gabber boys make the best 'shine in the Ozarks. It's a family tradition they've kept goin', and it's rumored there's more'n a few revenooers planted out on their property. Better let 'em know you ain't one, with you wearin' that CCC outfit and all."

I nodded. "Thanks."

He started shutting everything down then, and I fell into line behind him, thinking over what the old guy had said to me. Wiping down the counter and pop box while he took care of the cash register, I replayed the conversation in my mind.

We were outside locking down the pumps for the night when I said, "That Mr. Gabber wanted to know if I was being 'hurtful' with what I was writing. What in the hell did he mean by that?"

Pete shrugged. "Dunno. Guess he was looking out for his people. Folks around here got an awful lot of pride, mainly because most of 'em don't have a whole hell of a lot else."

"So he thought I might be making fun of them by telling their stories?"

"Maybe." Pete shrugged again.

"He told me a couple of other things. He said 'them folks' knew I was here, and that I didn't have to tell everything I heard. Who's 'them folks,' and what shouldn't I tell?"

He was getting in his green Hudson and at first I didn't think he heard me, because he shut the door and cranked the starter before answering. He was stalling again, thinking about what to say. So I just stood and waited, listening to the purr of the motor.

Finally, he rolled his window down. "I guess there ain't a town in the world without some kinda secrets they don't want let out," he said. "Folks who live in a place know its secrets, what to tell and what not to tell, and I guess they're just kinda juberous when someone they don't know comes in and starts diggin' 'round. Mackaville ain't no different. I know you, but they don't." He gave me a little salute. "Seeya tomorrow," he added, and roared off.

I stood there, watching him leave. Throughout the afternoon, big thick cumulus clouds had been piling up on the western horizon, darkening the tops of the green hills. It looked like my fellow traveler Mr. Clark was going to be right about the storm.

Sure enough, he was, as I told you at the beginning of this letter. But it wasn't the approaching storm that gave me the shivers as Pete drove down the little street and out of my sight. I was thinking that maybe I'd just been handed another piece or two of that damn jigsaw puzzle.

Your faithful correspondent,

Robert

May 28, 1939, Sunday morning

Dear John,

Thanks for your latest. It's good to know that you believe what I'm writing you, but I guess I wouldn't have expected any less. It's especially good that I got your letter Friday, the day after another... incident happened. You told me in your letter that you'd be the last person in the world to think I was crazy. This may cause you to re-evaluate your position.

I've been telling you about my problems with that big old calico cat. Well, since her visit last Monday night I've encouraged MacWhirtle to buddy up with me at night and he's been sleeping at the foot of my bed when he doesn't crawl over me and curl up in front of the window. Three nights ago, he and I finished off a box of Apple Snaps, which by the way are great cookies, and snuggled down.

I guess I'd been asleep for a few hours before I woke up, again with that same sense of dread I'd felt both times the cat had been in my room. I mean, I was soul-sick with fear, and as my consciousness raced up from deep sleep to high anxiety, I felt Mac's little body shaking against my stomach.

I was on my side facing the window, so I couldn't see the desk, but once again I could hear papers being scratched at and turned. As scared as I was, MacWhirtle seemed to be even worse. He was shaking so hard he was almost in convulsions.

That's what broke the spell for me. I just got mad as hell for that poor little dog. He'd trusted me, and I'd gotten him into <u>this</u>.

I was lying on my left arm, so I reached over with my right and gathered Mac in, stroking him. Boy, talk about a change! He stopped shaking and went rigid. My touch brought that dog out of it, and I got a little flash of insight: It was the <u>dog</u>, the dog and man working as a team, that brought humanity out of the caves and killed off the tigers and the bears. Mac may have just been a little rat terrier, but once he realized I was there with him, he was ready to kill bears just like his ancestors.

Suddenly, he jumped, making a strange noise that sounded for all the world like a Great Dane or even a wolf, clambering over my side and launching himself toward my desk. I twisted around just in time to see him hit the cat as it was turning to go.

The room exploded as though it had <u>ten</u> dogs and cats in it. Mac and the calico wrapped up together and hit the wall, bouncing to the floor in a clinch, and I could tell immediately that Mac was out for the kill. His barks were as high-pitched as screams. On top of that, he was growling like nothing his size is supposed to sound like as the two animals, wrapped together in a writhing, spitting mass, blasted from the floor up the side of my bed and over me, yowling and scratching and screaming, the cat and dog hair flying around in clouds. I'd gotten the lamp on above my bed and I scrunched up against the headboard, trying to get out of the way of the teeth and claws. In a twinkling, they'd fallen off the other side of the bed, and I could hear Mac's teeth snapping together. He was in a rage, fired in part by the fact that he'd been badly frightened. I know enough about dogs to guess that part of his motivation was his thinking he had to save me.

I had that big H&R break-over .22 revolver out from under my pillow and I was jumping around, trying to get off a shot that might hit the cat without hurting Mac. I guess I was shouting, too. I was afraid he'd be maimed or even killed, and it would be my fault.

Managing somehow to pull away from Mac, the big cat, looking very much chewed, jumped atop my desk. "Got you, you bastard," I thought, and I was just about to pump a round or two into her when she somehow just *wasn't there* any more and a woman's voice shouted,

"MAC! STOP THAT! STOP IT!"

As God is my witness, John, it came from behind that desk. And then – a *face* rose up. Or maybe just the impression of a face, if that makes any sense at all. It was an old woman's face, and it was agitated, staring daggers at Mac – and then at me.

Everything happened in a flash then. Mac, who was just about to leap, froze dead in his tracks. I was so startled I dropped the pistol. The face shimmered and was gone, and I thought I heard the cat's body bump on the floor outside my door, which would've meant it had gone through the transom again. Grabbing up my gun, I bolted out into the hall, Mac at my heels.

The cat was nowhere to be seen. There was a little fur on the hallway carpet. That was it.

Mac and I looked at each other. He whined softly, once. Then there was a thumping on the stairs, and Ma Stean appeared. As soon as she saw me, her eyes widened and I realized I was in my BVDs.

"Sorry, Miz Stean," I said, trying to cover up my private area with my hands, momentarily forgetting I was holding a gun.

"What in the blue blazes—?"

Backing toward the door, I said quickly, "I'll explain everything. Just let me get some clothes on."

"I seen men in their underwear before," she said. "I mean how come you're all bloody? And you've got a gun out?"

"Sorry," I said again, throwing my pistol onto the bed. Then I looked down. When MacWhirtle had launched himself from my thigh, his claws had dug deep enough to draw blood, which now oozed out of my leg in several places.

I got myself to the bathroom, wet down a washcloth, and stuck it up against the scratches to stanch the blood. Through the door, I explained to Ma what had happened. What seemed to disturb her most was the sight of my .22 pistol. In a few moments, I heard a couple of other voices, Dave's and Mr. Clark's, asking her what was going on. I was sure playing hell with the sleep patterns of her boarders, and I worried that she might be mad enough about the gun and everything else to suggest I find other lodging. But she didn't make any threats and seemed to understand well enough why I'd been racing through the hall with a loaded pistol. So did the other two, although I thought I heard Mr. Clark grumble something about the Old West and Dave kept asking if I was sure I was ok.

MacWhirtle had stayed outside the bathroom door, and I suspect his rough-looking state helped convince them I was telling the truth. It didn't hurt that they all knew I'd had trouble with that cat before.

So, the excitement died down and everyone went back to bed, including me – and MacWhirtle, who stuck to me like glue the rest of the night.

But John, while I told them about the cat and its fight with MacWhirtle, I didn't tell them anything about the old lady's voice that stopped the deadly struggle at its height. And I damn sure didn't tell 'em that when I looked toward the source of the voice, I can swear that the person I saw was that hideous old Mrs. Davis, Patricia's grandmother. And then she was gone. And the cat was, too.

I still don't know what all this means, but I've got an idea what I'm going to do about it. I'll tell you next letter.

Your pal,

Robert

May 30, 1939, Tuesday night

Dear John,

I have been doing my research. This burg has a pretty good public library, and I snatched away several hours of my interview time on Monday in order to see what I could find on magic and the occult. The library's books aren't as detailed as what I have back home, but they told me most of what I needed to know to start fitting those jigsaw pieces together.

I have to admit to a bit of worry after I mailed you my last. So it means a lot to me to have you say again in your latest that I could tell you anything and you'd still not think I was losing my mind. I needed that reassurance, even though I know I'm not going crazy. Thank God you know it, too.

I've been thinking about that night in the sleet storm when we were driving back to St. Paul and I stopped and made you drive the car because of my crummy night vision. You didn't want to, but I insisted, and after about five miles with you at the wheel we ran into that big Negro voodoo man, standing right in the middle of the road. I would've run right into him. But you stopped, and even though we didn't know what to do next we let him in and he started talking about the blood of a chicken and how we were good witches from the north and kissed both our hands when we let him off down the road, under a bridge where he could stay dry. Remember?

Hell yes, of course you do. And that time in Minneapolis when we went looking for back issues of pulps in junk stores and I took you straight over to a box, pulled it down, and started taking books out – Spicy Detectives, Flying Carpets, Weird Tales. You knew I'd never been in that place before.

And at the Ironside Theatre in Hallock, that night they were giving away the shotgun between features, and I told you I was going to win it before the first movie even started. You remember what happened. Mr. Ironside reached in, drew out a ticket stub – and I've got that old Remington double-barrel 12-gauge with me right now, although it's not quite in the same shape as it was.

At first I said maybe it was a sixth sense, where I just got feelings about stuff that turned out to be true, but then you told me, no, it's beyond that, beyond just intuition. It's a seventh sense, you said. Now, I find myself thinking about what you told me, that I see certain things clearly – that it is more than just a hunch. Remember all of those experiments we did trying to prove it? We just about wore out that pack of playing cards. But you remember the results as well as I do. All we found out was that we couldn't predict when it would come on, but when it did it was something real and concrete.

This is real, John, even though I don't know

all the details yet. These stories about witches, the three separate meetings with the cat, this feeling I can't shake – it's all coalescing into something tangible and very, very big. I'm traveling from the sixth to the seventh sense now, and I don't know what's in store or how long the journey will be, but I am now convinced some crazy woman is changing herself into a cat or somehow projecting herself into a cat and going through my reports. She's <u>got</u> to be crazy because I've caught her three times and Mac the Killer Rat Dog ate her ass up the last time, Friday night, and if things had been just a little different I'd have blasted her to Hell myself.

I say she's crazy because I know she's coming back. Why? Because I <u>know</u>.

I couldn't guess the reason. All I've got is copies of a bunch of yarns from senile old poots talking about stuff that happened a hundred years ago. I've gone over all the stories I've sent to Washington so far and nothing's caught my eye. I've thought about sending you my carbons but I decided not to. If they somehow got lost in the mail I would be screwed because they're all I've got, with the originals all going to main office. I know I could try and make double carbons of every one so I could send copies to you, but it makes my fingers sore and half the time parts are so light you have to guess what the words are. So I'll save that for the ones I really think you need to see.

I've studied them all, though, especially the ones with witches, and my time in the library just reinforced my decision to do what I hinted I was going to do in my last letter. It involves that Remington double-barrel I won all those years ago at the picture show – the only weapon besides the H&R revolver I brought with me to Arkansas (although Ma Stean doesn't exactly know I have it here in my closet).

Maybe you remember: a silver bullet is the only thing that can kill a were-animal. I remembered, and I made sure I was right, or as right as you can be about something like this, by doing my research. A couple of the old books mentioned crucifixes, an image of the Madonna, or holy water. I didn't have any of those things, but I did have a couple of firearms, so that made my decision for me.

From the library, I walked back to Ma Stean's, wrapped up my shotgun in an old shirt, and drove it over to Pete's in the sidecar of the big Indian, hidden from curious eyes. It wasn't busy at Pete's and he grinned a hello as I came into the station office with my bundle, watched as I opened it to reveal the Remington.

"You plannin' on holdin' me up?" he asked, still grinning, his dark eyes going from me to the shotgun.

"Only if you don't cooperate," I said. "I need to cut this baby down. You got anything I can use?"

He nodded. "Yeh." Disappearing into the

back, he came back presently with a heavy-duty hacksaw. "This oughta do it."

I took it out to the back bay and went to work, clamping the barrel in a vise and starting out a foot from the end. Pete followed me out and watched as I started sawing.

"You sure are screwin' up a good shotgun," he observed.

"Yeah, and I'm going to screw up a big calico cat even more."

"A cat? What th' hell for?"

I kept sawing away as I talked. "You'll think I'm nuts," I said, wishing I hadn't mentioned anything about the cat.

"Try me," he said.

I looked back at him. The smile was gone.

It was my turn to clam up and think before I said anything else. I'd told him a few stories about the crap you and I used to get into back in Hallock, but I hadn't really broached the subject of magic or the supernatural, and certainly not anything about the seventh sense.

I sawed silently until a good inch of metal clunked to the floor of the bay and I took a file to the rough spots left at the end of the barrel, still not looking at Pete. Finally, I thought, what the hell?

"All right," I told him, looking up. "I'm after a were-cat."

He'd just fired up a Spud cigarette. Now, he took it out of his mouth. Maybe I expected him to laugh, but he didn't.

"What the hell is that?" he asked slowly.

"And why the hell do you think you have to kill it?"

Before I knew it, I was telling him the whole story. I didn't think he was buying any of it at first. Like I wrote you earlier, he looks like my Uncle Chuck, with a hooked nose and droopy eyelids, and that kind of face can be hard to read. But as I talked, I guess he could see I wasn't making it up, because, "I vas dere, Charley!"

"So," I concluded, "the next time she comes back, I'm going to blast her. I've had it."

He knocked a long ash off his fag and shook his head.

"What you're gonna do is blast holes in Miz Stean's walls, maybe kill a cat, and get your dumb Yankee ass thrown in jail," he said. Although he didn't raise his voice, it was clear to me that he didn't approve.

"Look," I began. "You haven't been scared shitless by this thing. I have. I'm just defending myself."

Reaching into the front pocket of my uniform, I pulled out about a dollar's worth of dimes. There was an anvil on the work bench and a ball-peen hammer nearby. Sprinkling four or five dimes on top of the anvil, I started in hammering them as flat as I could get them.

"Got any tin snips?" I asked.

"Sure." He reached into a drawer beside the bench and handed them over.

I began cutting away at the dimes. The snips

were sharp, so it was fast work. Pete watched, saying nothing, until I'd finished.

"Mind if I ask why you cut up them perfectly good dimes? You know you can't spend 'em now."

"Sure," I returned. "I'm gonna load 'em in a couple of shotgun shells."

"So they'll be..." he paused.

"Yeah. Silver bullets."

Man, did I get a reaction! "NO!" he shouted. Moving faster than I'd ever seen him, he swept his hand across the top of the anvil, scattering the cut-up dimes across the work table and onto the floor.

"Pete," I said, shocked. "What the hell... ?"

His eyes weren't drooping any more. They were wild and flashing. Grabbing me by the shoulders, he almost shouted, "No, no, you can't do it. You can't do it. You can't kill an old lady who hasn't harmed you."

"Pete, what—"

"She's just protectin' the others, man. You can't kill her." He was so upset that I couldn't follow what he was saying, but he held onto me and kept after it. I didn't know what the hell was going on, but it scared me to see him this way.

"All right," I kept saying, because it was all I knew to say. "All right. I'm just bullshitting you, Pete. I won't kill that cat. I won't. Honest."

He stopped raving then, staring at me like a disturbed animal.

"Relax," I said. "I'm just blowing. I'm not going to shoot that cat. You're right. I'd just mess up Ma Stean's walls, or maybe blow my own foot off."

Gradually, he let go of my shoulders. His face still close to mine, he said, "You sure you ain't gonna shoot her?"

"I'm not. I just want her to leave me and Mac alone. Three times now she's come into my room. I don't know what it is she's looking for, but I'd be glad to give it to her if she'd just stay the hell away."

"You mean that?"

John, I still didn't know what was going on. I was communicating on pure instinct. Maybe something more.

"Sure," I said. "I just want to be able to get some sleep. That's all."

In a second, he was back to his old self. He'd dropped his Spud on the floor, and he bent down to pick it up.

"Damn it," he said. "Got grease on it. Shit."

He pulled the pack out of his shirt pocket and shook out another, lighting it thoughtfully with a Zippo, not looking at me. He took his time, and I knew he was thinking again.

"Tell you what," he said finally. "You give me a chance, I think I can — I may be able to help. I mean, well, I think I know what all this is about."

It was my turn to be incredulous. "You mean

with that cat? That were-cat or whatever the hell it is?"

"Yeah." He took a deep drag. "Look, go on down to Foreman's Drug and have a Coke. Give me thirty minutes and then go back to Miz Stean's. If you get tied up there, don't worry about getting back here this evening. I'll manage without you."

I nodded. "I'm sorry," I said. "I didn't mean to upset you. I don't know—"

"No," he interrupted, "you don't. But you'll know more after tonight."

I didn't know what else to do but sweep up the silver, say thanks, and leave, rattled as I was. And I know this is turning into a magnum opus, but I have to tell you what happened next.

I hiked off down to Foreman's feeling pretty strange. Pete's reaction had been one of real and touching concern for – who? Or what? – a cat? A were-cat? Pete was the only real pal I had in town and the way all the evidence pointed, he was somehow in league with a pussycat who could read and who'd been scaring hell out of me and Mac. This is starting to sound like a cartoon horror story told by Leon Schlesinger or Walt Disney. I tell you, I was feeling like you did in the Sophia incident. Hell, you remember. Soofeeyah, that little black-haired, deep-eyed, huge-bazoomed frail you had such a crush on. I didn't know her, but I did the old "mind-reading" trick on her from afar and told you she liked you and she wanted something from you I couldn't quite figure out. You went for broke and asked her, and when she told you it got us as close to a fight as we'd ever gotten. What she wanted, as you well remember, was an introduction to <u>me</u>.

You didn't believe me – you probably still don't – but I really didn't have any idea that was what she wanted from you.

I have to grin even now, thinking about it, but that is also what's happening with Pete and me. I never picked up on Pete knowing anything about the cat. I'd never said anything to him about it before last Monday. It came right out of the blue, just like Soofeeyah's crush on me.

So I spent thirty minutes at the drug store with a nickel cherry phosphate and walked on back to Ma Stean's, my Indian still parked at Pete's Skelly station. The only car in the drive was Ma's old Pontiac touring sedan, and my heart kind of sank. Everything seemed quiet. I guessed Pete had not been able to fix anything up after all.

Mac came running out when I stepped up on the porch, barking his little head off to let the world know I was home, and then zipped back into the living room. <u>That's odd</u>, I thought. Usually once I was there he stuck right to my side.

I opened the screen door and stepped into the foyer – and suddenly my skin prickled like someone had hosed me down with ice water! At the same time, I heard a voice from Ma's living room.

"Mac! Get down! You're just trying to be nice to me – but I know what you did!" The voice was old and without rancor, and when I followed it into the room I was suddenly looking into the near-translucent eyes of Old Lady Davis, Patricia's ugly grandma. Ma Stean was sitting on the sofa just behind her, and MacWhirtle was at Grandma Davis's feet, tail wagging wildly.

"Excuse me, Mrs. Stean," I said. "I didn't know you had company."

Waves of goose pimples seemed to wash over me as I looked from her to Mrs. Davis. At the same time, I thought it funny that the old woman didn't look quite as repulsive as I remembered.

"Come in, Mr. Brown," Ma said with a smile. "I was just telling Mrs. Davis about you."

I took her withered hand and smiled. "It is a pleasure to finally make your acquaintance," I said. "We've met, but not formally."

"Yes." She nodded. "At Mr. Barlow's filling station. Nice to see you again, young man."

The mention of Pete's name triggered something. At that moment, I knew she was the one I was supposed to meet here. And in a twinkling, I knew what I had to do. Knew it.

"Mrs. Davis," I began. "And Ma – Mrs. Stean – may I ask a favor of you?" Neither spoke, but their faces told me to go on.

"I work for the WPA, as you know, Ma. I talk to people around here and write up stories they tell me. It's part of a project to save early tales of folklore before all the people who know them are dead and gone. What I want to know is if you ladies would mind taking a look-see at what I've written so far."

I paused, for effect as much as anything. "You see, I'm worried that something I've written could cause embarrassment or even distress to someone, and that's the last thing I want."

Mrs. Davis looked kind of funny as I bulled on.

"You both have lived around here and would know if I wrote something I shouldn't. I know it's an imposition, but there's not that much. If you'll wait right here, I'll go get it. Everything."

I turned and hurried out of the room, feeling like I was going to catch a bullet in my back. Ma said something, but I had scooted out of earshot before she finished. Pounding up the stairs and down the hall to my room, I scooped up all my reports, rough drafts, and note books and raced back. I wasn't even breathing hard when I reached the living room and deposited the stack on the coffee table in front of the sofa.

It didn't seem that impressive, John. Most of the stories go only three or four type-written pages, a few as much as five or six, but it was a small stack any way you looked at it. I got down on my knees beside the table and quickly sorted the papers into three piles:

interviews sent in, interviews to be sent, and notes and drafts in incomplete form.

I looked up. Neither Mrs. Davis nor Ma Stean had moved or said a word. "This is it," I said. "Everything. Do you mind?"

The old lady actually smiled. It's going to sound corny to you, but at that moment she did not look ugly at all.

" 'Course not," she said.

Then Mac came over and stood right next to me, looking up at Mrs. Davis. It was like I was seeing her through his eyes, and I knew that finally I was going to be able to put together a little bit of the jigsaw, maybe a border to anchor the other pieces to.

But that's going to have to wait. Hell, it's almost midnight, I'm written out, and that bed looks damn good – especially when I feel sure there won't be any visiting felines tonight. Mac feels the same way; even with me typing away, he's been asleep on the bed for hours.

Tomorrow, I promise, I'll give you the rest. Right now I'm just beat.

Your pal through it all,

Robert

May 31, 1939, Wednesday night

Dear John,

Since I got behind on my work on Monday, thanks to doing research at the library and everything that happened with Pete acting so crazy and my finding Mrs. Davis at the boarding house and deciding to lay things out with her and Ma – well, I've been having to kind of go lickety-split to catch up. The only thing interesting (maybe that's the wrong word) about my interviews lately is what happened today when I was coming home after taking down still another whiskery old tale of how grandmammy and grandpappy lived in those ancient times of the 1800s, etc. I'll tell you about the "interesting" part at the end of this letter if I still have the pep.

But first, what I promised you – the rest of the story about Mrs. Davis and Ma and what I decided to do around Monday noon.

You may wonder why I did what I did. Well, I thought – no, I knew – that it was what I was supposed to do, if you get me. Sure as hell, I knew that Pete had sent me down to Foreman's Drug so he could get hold of Mrs. Davis and tell her to get over to Ma's. He'd told me, you remember, that I'd "know more after tonight."

And now I damn sure do.

I was going on seventh-sense instinct when I decided to show those two ladies my notes and interviews. Like I wrote, I was looking for a few border pieces of the Mackaville jigsaw, just to get a good start on the scene that I can feel deep into my bones but not yet see. When Pete went into a fit and scattered those dimes, I knew he was a part of it. And you know I already had my suspicions about Mrs. Davis. I couldn't say for certain it was her I'd heard and half-seen when I was about to shoot that son-of-a-bitching cat a few nights ago – it sure didn't seem like the same person I met in Ma Stean's sitting room, although maybe a little more like the strange old woman Patricica brought in the car to Pete's station – but I <u>felt</u> it. And I also felt, somehow, that maybe everything would come together if I did the right things. Something told me one of those right things was laying every card I had out on the table, face up. And that meant to let Mrs. Davis and Ma see everything I'd done.

Although she tried not to act eager, I couldn't help but notice that Mrs. Davis sat right down on the sofa, took out a pair of big glasses, and started poring over my material. I wasn't sure whether to stay or leave, and Ma must've sensed my uncertainty, because she said, "It's pert near lunchtime, but ain't none of the other boys gonna be in today. How 'bout I fix you up a ham sandwich now?" And she motioned me toward the dining room. I think I told you MacWhirtle was there and he followed me in and sat there, just nakedly begging for a little of whatever I got to eat.

It felt funny to be the only one sitting

there at the big table designed to accommodate all Ma's boarders – funny and kind of empty. I thanked Ma when she sat the plate and a big glass of milk in front of me, then watched her as she disappeared back into the room where Mrs. Davis was examining my documents. As I ate, slipping MacWhirtle a pinch or two of ham from inside the thick-sliced bread, I could hear one or the other of them chuckle every once in a while when they saw a name they knew. They knew pretty much every one.

"Looky there, it's Ginny Groff. Wonder if there's anything in there about how shiftless her gran'pa was?" That was Ma's voice.

Then, Mrs. Davis. "I'd forgotten about Old Clem Hardage, Mildred's papa. He was a character, weren't he?"

And so on. I forced myself to eat slowly as I listened, eavesdropping, wanting to let them give it all a good going-over before I came back out. They'd make comments, point things out to one another, and occasionally fall silent for a few moments. John, you don't have to ask me how I know that when they stopped talking, they'd gotten to one of the scary stories, the witch stories, or something else that really grabbed their attention. They knew I was listening, and when they stopped talking I could almost see them nodding knowingly at one another as they both looked over some piece of paper.

I sat there as long as I could, antsy, knowing I had an interview coming up with a married couple in their seventies who lived close enough to town to have a home telephone. I thought about calling and rescheduling, but then another idea hit me like a lightning bolt and I got up from the table and walked into the living room.

You wrote that you believed me when I talked about the cat looking at the notes and all that jazz. I hope you'll believe me now when I tell you that what to do just <u>came</u> to me, like it was someone else inside my head giving me directions. That's happened before a few times, but never as powerfully as it did this time.

The two ladies looked up when I came in. Maybe they saw something in my eyes. They seemed to be waiting for what I had to say – almost like they knew beforehand.

"Thank you for the sandwich, Ma," I said. "I've got to go out to the Rayfords in just a little bit – I'm sure you know 'em – but I wanted to tell you both something first."

Ma nodded. Mrs. Davis looked at me expectantly.

"Somehow, I think you'll understand this. A lot of people wouldn't." I swallowed.

Suddenly, it felt as though there were a noose around my throat. What if it was wrong for me to be saying what I was getting ready to say? What if Mrs. Davis got up and left? What if Ma threw me out? What if something <u>worse</u> happened? What if? <u>What if</u>?

<u>The hell with it</u>, I thought. I plunged ahead.

"I've got kind of a gift. I've had it ever since I was a kid. Some say I got it from my grandmother, my mother's mother, who had a lot of strange notions and strange... powers, I guess you'd say. It's what I call a seventh sense, because I think it's a little different than a sixth sense. It goes further than just getting hunches you can't explain that turn out to be right. My seventh sense, or whatever you want to call it, isn't with me all the time, but when it is, I can see things and feel things that most people don't ever see or feel."

I tried to read what was in their eyes, hoping that they didn't think I was just full of shit or loony. A lot depended on this next minute or two.

Neither said a word.

I fixed my gaze on Mrs. Davis. "I've awakened to find a big calico cat in my room for three nights now, as Ma can tell you. And I'm sure all that cat wanted was to read the notes you've got right there before you." I paused, not wanting to go too far. "I'm not sure why an animal would have any interest in that, but I've got my suspicions. And I also think, well, that now that you've seen what I've written, Mrs. Davis, I'm not going to have any trouble with that cat any more."

Ma got up. " 'Scuse me," she said, and headed toward the dining room I'd just vacated, leaving me with Mrs. Davis. Had she heard enough? Or was she leaving me alone with Patricia's grandmother so the old lady could tell me what she wanted to tell me in private?

If I expected the latter, I was wrong. Mrs. Davis didn't start talking after Ma was out of sight. She just sat there, meeting my gaze with a steady one of her own, the corners of her mouth crinkled up a little.

"Maybe Ma thinks I'm cuckoo," I said. "Maybe you do, too. I hope not."

"I don't know as I'd be worryin' about that," she said.

"All right, I won't. So I'll just lay it right out. I don't know how or why or anything else, but I feel like you and that cat, what that cat did, are somehow related." I paused to let that sink in.

"Mebbe you been takin' down too many witch stories," she said, not in an unkind way. A flicker of a smile played across her lips.

"It's possible. But you know Pete Barlow, and when he found out I was cutting up dimes to put in shotgun shells to go after that cat, he went a little nuts. And he called you, and here we are."

"Well," she said, and it was more statement than question.

"Please know I don't mean to offend you, but I think maybe what that cat wanted to know was what I planned to do about that state registrar's letter – you saw it in the stack, didn't you?"

"I did."

"About reporting people who were 'passing for white?'"

This time, she just nodded.

"Well," I said, going to the sheaf of papers and leafing through until I found the letter, "here's what I'm going to do about it." And I tore up the letter and the envelope right in front of her, dropping the pieces into the wastebasket.

"It's not my damn – excuse me, Mrs. Davis – darn business to report on the color of peoples' skin," I said. "I'm pretty sure that most people in this town have some Negro blood, but I'm a damn – excuse me again – Northerner and that doesn't bother me one bit."

"You're telling me the truth?" she asked.

"I am. And you can tell the cat the same thing."

This time, she did grin. "Well, on behalf of the town, I'm much obliged to you."

"You're welcome. I didn't mean to be pushy, but I was pretty sure that's one of the things the cat was looking for in my papers. I think there's something else, too, something I'm not sure about yet."

"That right?"

"Yes."

Her eyes narrowed a little, her grin fading. "What is it?"

Then, unbidden, the question just pushed its way up and out. Believe me, John, it wasn't what I planned to say. I was going to be a lot more subtle, see if I could work it out of her. Instead, it just came out.

"What was the 'cleansing?' " I asked.

I have to give it to that old lady. I could see that the question hit her like a cannonball to the chest. Hell, John, she even flinched. Physically. But her face, her eyes, didn't move, and her voice was steady when she spoke.

"Where on earth you hear about <u>that</u>?"

I told her about the colored place I'd been to with Pete and Duffy. I didn't see any reason not to. And I knew Ma was listening from inside the dining room, too, just like I'd done when the two of them looked over my notes.

"The old man spoke about the jubilee and the cleansing. I know that a jubilee is usually a 50-year anniversary, but I just put in a good amount of time at the library, and the only jubilee I found for this year that made any sense was the Oklahoma Land Run, back in 1889, that opened up your neighboring state. A big deal, but I don't think that's it."

I locked eyes with Mrs. Davis, who didn't speak, didn't move. In the silence, I could hear Ma bustling around in the other room. She didn't fool me.

"No," she finally said, getting up from the sofa. "That ain't it."

"Then you know?"

She sighed then. "I know more'n I can tell. Like every place, this town's got its secrets, and it don't want no one stirrin' into 'em." She looked at me, and I could swear I saw something like affection in her eyes. "I don't imagine that'll stop you, though. Just watch out. You won't have any more trouble with that old calico, but there's lots worse animals than cats out there."

"Animals?" I asked.

She headed toward the door. "Yeah. Just keep your eyes open," she said. "And watch your feet."

Watch your feet? Where had I heard _that_ before?

"So you're not going to tell me about the cleansing?"

"Not right now," she said over her shoulder.

"Maybe later? Maybe I can come see you?"

"Maybe." She paused at the door. "Or maybe you just want to visit me 'cause my granddaughter might be there." Grinning now, she added, "You ain't the only one who can see things."

And then, John, I swear that those big hazel eyes of hers turned yellow and the pupils went vertical, like egg yolks sliced with a piece of charcoal. It froze my blood. I knew she was looking inside me like that cat had looked at my notes, trying to read whatever was there.

Suddenly, Mac yipped, breaking the spell. I looked down to see him at my feet, and when my gaze went back to Mrs. Davis, her eyes had returned to normal. Mac looked up at me as though to say, _Did you see that_?

I know. I _know_.

Ma came out of the kitchen then and walked

Mrs. Davis out of the house. I sure would've liked to know what they were saying to one another, but apparently my seventh sense didn't go that far because I came up with nothing except a big load of the creepy feeling that's been with me more and more as I go through my life in this strange little burg.

Thinking about all of that, I almost forgot to tell you what happened a few hours ago, when I was coming down out of the hills after interviewing an old man named Bird, who mostly talked about what a swell feller his grandpa was back in the old days. As I went around a curve up on Mount Howard Road, with about a thousand-foot drop on one side of me and woods on the other, someone threw a log at me. Maybe from up in a tree or from a hillside. It thudded and skidded in front of the big Indian and I had to swerve to miss it. So I'm still here. And thinking a lot about who might've pitched that lumber.

Funny. Right about the same time, I'd been mulling over what Mrs. Davis had said about watching my feet, trying to dope out where I'd heard those exact words before. And just as I remembered it was one of those damn Black twins from the train station — bang! Here came the log.

Coincidence? I don't know if I believe in those anymore.

Slept good Monday and Tuesday night. And even though somebody (I'm just pretty damn sure it was of those idiot Blacks) tried to knock me off the road a couple of hours ago, I'm bushed and ready to fall into bed for a rest that I know will be cat-free, unless I find that calico curled up in the arms of Morpheus.

Your pal,

Robert

June 3, 1939, a warm Saturday afternoon

Dear John,

I've been thinking about these letters I'm sending and I've got a couple of things I want to tell you: 1. Keep them so I can read them when I come back to Minnesota for Christmas, and 2. Don't expect me to write long hair-raising passages. I'll tell you about the scary stuff when it happens but you must understand the reasons for these priceless literary gems. They're written to let you know what's going on, so if anything happens they won't be able to just throw my body in a bar ditch and pretend I just disappeared and they haven't the faintest notion of where I went. (Who's "they?" Hell if I know.) I'm also writing them to calm myself down and remind myself that my best friend ever since ninth grade is out there rooting for me. That's why I spend time telling you about my job and the people as well as the weird things that have been happening.

A few days ago, when I laid it on the line with Mrs. Davis and Ma Stean, I really had some misgivings. I think whatever wild seventh-sense talent I have, those weird little flashes of precognition or knowing what someone is thinking/feeling/going to do, could easily be getting my ass into a heap of trouble here. Anybody else in my shoes would just be writing up the folklore, laughing off the occasional witch story, and having a good time. Then they'd leave and go on to something else and that would be all there was to it.

I wish I could do that. But because I know, I've got to dig deeper. I'm going to try to be careful, but I will figure out this whole thing with the jubilee and the cleansing, even though I'm more uneasy, maybe even frightened, than I want to admit. Telling you all about it helps a lot, and knowing that you believe what I write helps even more.

Ok, now that I've said all that, things have been pretty quiet for a change. Summer's here, and even as lush and green as this place is it still gets plenty hot. Got a good breeze this morning and that helps some. Can't smell the stockyards.

So all's quiet on the Southern front. No more old calico to wake me up in the night, and thanks to Mrs. Davis I don't think there ever will be again. You can draw your own conclusions about her relationship with that cat. I've already drawn mine, but I haven't shared them with anyone, not even Pete, who I know is involved in the whole thing. In fact, he hasn't said a word about it since he got me and Mrs. Davis together, and for now it seems right to follow his lead.

This morning I took the motorbike up into the mountains and did a little stunting. I love that old Indian bike and for a guy who never drove one before I'm doing pretty good. It's heavy but powerful and I can pull the hills and mountain trails without a hesitation. Fact is,

I can do fifty uphill, and out here, boy, uphill means UP.

What I did today was something I call "rimming." The WPA has put in lots of new roads around Mackaville and they "crown" the roads toward the side of the hill or mountain. That means the roads slant away from the outer edge, which runs above everything from a ten-foot to a thousand-foot drop. What they did was build something like a little bitty sidewalk about a foot wide over the outer edge, a lip – like curbing – that's turned up on the outside. This structure is supposed to help keep the gravel roads together, with the lip there to bump your wheels back from the edge if you get too close.

Rimming is a motorbike sport I invented once I got a little more confident about riding the big Indian. When I start down a mountainside, I'll go as fast as I can, lean way over to the uphill side, and balance the bike up onto the top of the lip. I can really roar down a hill, sometimes seventy or eighty miles an hour. While it sounds risky, it still gives you an unmatched thrill, plus you cover ground a lot faster.

With the side car on, it's even better. I found that I can lean over so far that the side car is actually out in space, acting kind of like an outrigger. Its weight really allows me to pile on some speed. Because my vision's not top-notch, as you well know, I really have to be alert for the drains, which are little cut-outs in the lip for the rainwater to flow into.

I suspect if I hit one of those in just the wrong way I would get a free and brief flying lesson as I cannoned out into space off the mountainside.

I got on an old logging road last week that seemed really smooth. When I came back from one of my interviews I stopped at the top of it. Because of all the big trucks the loggers use, there aren't many hard turns in logging roads (something I just learned), so I put my goggles on, buttoned my leather jacket, and let 'er rip! I roared down that mountain, the old bike vibrating and bouncing – one bounce I know cleared 20 feet – and, this is the climax, I hit a hundred miles an hour (or so close to it that it doesn't matter – the Indian's speedometer doesn't work all that well). Man oh man, what a thrill!

Although it registers much lower on the thrill docket, I did get notice from the government that I'm now officially a GS-1. So technically, I've started a new (same old) job. Wonder if we rich federal executives get paid at a different time of the month? Guess I'll find out soon enough. If nothing else, it'll be nice to throw away that little note book Uncle Sam's made me carry, and not have to put notations in it about every cent I've spent in the line of duty.

I'm going to the garage in a little bit and help Pete for a while, as per our agreement, then I'm picking up Patricia on the Indian, putting her in the sidecar, and heading to the

Palace, the top picture show (of two) here in town. Yes, I finally got up the courage and asked her out – not face to face, but over the 'phone one evening. I didn't even call her from the boarding house, because I didn't want anyone hearing me, just in case she turned me down. So Wednesday evening, just as Pete went out to gas up a car, I called the Davis residence from the gas-station's office – and I got lucky, because Patricia herself answered the phone. While keeping an eye on Pete, I blurted out the invite, and damned if she didn't accept. Although you know how I love the B-movies and would've been very happy going to the Maribel and seeing Wolf Call, with John Carroll (the poor man's Clark Gable), a Monogram special, and some horse opera called Songs and Saddles, starring – get this – Gene Austin, that crooner who did tunes like "My Blue Heaven" and "I Dream of Lilac Time" a hundred years ago (or at least ten). But I got the idea she'd rather go to the nicer movie house, and that's jake with me. So we agreed on the Palace, which is showing a single, big-studio feature: Jesse James with Tyrone Power.

To tell you the truth, I wanted to take her to the Gem, that big impressive movie house in Harrison where I saw Robin Hood with Pete and Duffy a couple of weeks ago, but she told me her grandmother doesn't want her going out of town on a date, so I didn't press the issue. I'm beginning to like that old lady, and the more I think about it the more I know she holds some kind of key that just might unlock the box of secrets this town has stored up.

I just looked back on this letter, and I see up until now I haven't said anything new about the cleansing or the jubilee. That's because there's not a thing to report on either subject. I haven't felt like the time is right to broach Mrs. Davis again on the subject, and while I think both Ma and Pete know a lot more than they're letting on, I'm not comfortable about asking them, either. I could tell you that I have a feeling something's about to happen, and that I also feel like Mrs. Davis wants to let me find out a little more for myself before she tells me anything else. For whatever reason, she maybe wants me to work for it. And to work for Patricia, for that matter.

One more thing, John. If anything happens to me, I want you to have any of my books or pulp magazines you want. Not that I think anything's going to happen, but I think something could. If it does, show this paragraph to my folks and then take what you want from my bookshelf.

Your faithful comrade,

Robert

June 4, 1939, Sunday morning

Dear John,

Well, I don't want to kiss and tell. Oh hell – yes, I do. I kissed Patricia last night, right on the damn lips, before I walked her to her door. There was a nice moon out, and she looked up at me as I was helping her out of the sidecar, moonlight in her eyes, and I kissed her.

It was like being in a movie. That's all I can say.

Before that, when I went to pick her up at her house just on the outskirts of town, Mrs. Davis let me in and had me sit down in their old-fashioned parlor. She even brought me lemonade. While I waited for Patricia, we talked about different things, even how my work was going, but none of the conversation went very deep, if you know what I mean. She did ask me how old I was – wondering, I guess, if I was some sort of cradle-robber, and seemed satisfied to find out I was only a few years older than her granddaughter. The house is a two-story, old but solid, and it's immaculate, right down to the crisp white doilies on the overstuffed chairs.

When I complimented her on the place, she smiled and said, "Rupert – Mister Davis – builded most of it hisself, and he builded it to last. He took good care of me before he passed."

"I'm sorry to hear that, Miz Davis."

"It's been a long while now," she said.

I felt then just a twinge of the old seventh sense. Maybe that's what made me ask what I knew was an improper question.

"How did your husband die, Miz Davis?"

She hesitated just a moment before answering. "Cholera," she said. "An epidemic. Got a lot of folks around these parts."

"When?"

She looked at me, and the pain from his death still seemed to be flickering in her eyes. "A long time ago, Mister Brown," she said. "We was awful young."

Just about that time, Patricia made her entrance, coming down the stairs looking just a little self-conscious in a dress as blue as a robin's egg, which made a real pleasant contrast with the coffee-and-cream color of her skin. She really is good-looking.

So we saw the movie, and it was damn good. Big budget, big actors, and a big story, all in Technicolor. Even the short subjects were top-notch: "Daffy Duck in Hollywood" and "Pie A La Maid," a Charley Chase short in which a waitress falls for Charley because she thinks he's a gangster. The newsreel had a little too much about the crazy little dictator in Germany to suit me, but other than that it was all aces.

Well, maybe I thought it was better than it was because I had Patricia sitting next to me. As long as she was there, I could watch paint dry and be happy for the experience. A bunch of her teenaged friends were there, too, and they gave me the eye pretty good, especially the guys. I let 'em look. We may have been in some small-town picture show, but I was sitting on top of the world.

After I let Patricia off – the porch light was on, so I thought it best not to try for another kiss – I didn't feel like going back to Ma's quite yet. Since the lights on the old motorbike are in good working shape now, I figured maybe I'd just ride out in the mountains for a little while. But then I thought of something and changed my plans. Instead of shooting off into the countryside, I headed back up through town toward the railroad station and the cemetery. Hard to believe it'll be a month ago tomorrow since I first rolled into town and saw that calico cat for the first time, sitting atop that crypt watching the train.

Now, I realized what I was planning to do was kind of a shot in the dark, but I didn't have anything else to occupy me at that hour but reading or sleeping, and I didn't really want to do either one. Instead, I had a feeling again, like I was back on the trail of something.

Little towns like Mackaville always seem to take good care of their dead. The cemeteries are generally well-kept, free from debris and weeds, and from what I could tell in the dark, this one seemed to be no exception. It was pretty big, too, big enough that I didn't know where to start.

So I just used my instinct. My seventh sense.

It didn't happen right away. I played the beam of my big flashlight over a lot of tombs and headstones before I found what I was looking for. I figured I'd hit pay dirt when I started seeing stones with the last name of Davis – which is a common enough surname, sure, but in a small place like this most of the Davises were probably related and the late ones buried near each other, connected in death as well as life.

But while there were about a dozen Davises buried there, I couldn't find any stone for a Rupert Davis.

I started thinking maybe I'd heard Mrs. Davis wrong and her husband's first name was something different. As I pursued that line of reasoning, I kept idly shining my flashlight over other stones, not really looking at them.

Then, I saw it, off to one side, a few scraggly bushes growing up around it.

John, this tombstone was <u>huge</u>. Five or six times the size of a regular marker, it looked like a stone wall jutting up out of the ground – rectangular, the front angled backward maybe 40 degrees, all apparently cut out of one big slab of granite. On closer examination, I saw neat lines of names, dozens of them, probably close to two hundred, each with a year beside it. At the very top, two-inch-high lettering was chiseled into the stone: ALL DIED 1889.

So these were the victims of the cholera epidemic, and the years were the dates of their birth. I ran my light down the rows of lettering, recognizing several surnames from my interviews. Then I found the one I was looking for.

Like I wrote earlier, there was nearly a full moon in the sky last night, but it didn't give the same effect in the bone yard that it had an hour or so earlier, reflected in Patricia's eyes. I know. I'm starting to sound like a narrator out of Ranch Romances or Love Story. But the setting had gone from love-pulp moonlight to the ghostly lumination in a Weird Tales yarn. I felt goosebumps rising as I focused on the name and date.

RUPERT DAVIS — 1858.

I did a little mental arithmetic. If Mrs. Davis was 75 years old now, which I figured was in the ballpark, she would've been only around 25 when her husband was cut down. That would have made her about five years younger than him — the same number of years between Patricia and me.

I thought about that a minute while my light danced around his name and the other names, all chiseled in the stone monolith. Then it hit me like a splash of ice water.

ALL DIED 1889.

Eighteen eighty-nine. Fifty years ago. The jubilee?

I'm getting the chills now, as I type this in my comfortable second-floor room, well away from that resting ground of the dead. Because what I encountered next wasn't dead at all. There was a rustling behind me, and I whipped around and shone my flashlight on – cats. A couple dozen, at least, climbing out from behind crypts and stones and from God knows where else, lining up like little animal soldiers, all of them staring right at me.

And then, the old calico. She appeared out of the darkness, walking through the line those animals had formed, not stopping, coming on her cat's feet toward me, closer and closer, stopping so close to me that her front claws almost touched the toe of my left boot.

And dammit, John, she looked at me. And nodded.

Truthfully,

Robert

June 6, 1939, Tuesday evening

Dear John,

I know I left you hanging with my last letter and I apologize. It's taken me a couple of days of heavy thinking just to come to terms with what went on that Saturday night. I'm not sure I believe it myself. A cat nodded at me? What's the old saying? Dogs look up at you and cats look down on you? This cat didn't do either – she looked right <u>at</u> me, like a human being would do.

I guess I was kind of in shock after all of that, because the next thing I knew they had all disappeared, gone back wherever they came from. Once she'd marched up to me and gave her nod, the calico had turned and walked away. I could see she was still a little worse for wear after her dustup with MacWhirtle; a big patch of fur was gone from her right haunch, the skin raw and scratched up. Still, she carried herself regally past the massed felines there in the dead of night. I saw it with only moonlight to illuminate the scene; somewhere in there, I'd forgotten about the flashlight in my hand, and it was pointing straight down, beaming a moon-shaped tight spot on the ground, when I remembered I held it. By the time I had the presence of mind to throw some light around the cemetery, the animals had gone, leaving me to wonder if it had been some sort of vision or eyes-open dream.

Anyway, I'll tell the world I got the hell out of there.

It's been almost three days now, and I've been working pretty hard at my job, which helps me not to dwell all the time on this town's crazy mysteries – although I'm still keeping my eyes open, convinced more than ever that I'm on the verge of something.

For a change of pace, I'll tell you a little more about the work I'm doing.

When I go out, I have with me a letter of introduction from the White House, signed by President Roosevelt. I'll bet it's really signed by a machine, but it impresses the locals. (There's been one or two, not many, that hate FDR and didn't mind telling me so, but I managed to interview them anyway – all except for one old geezer who threatened to unload a shotgun on my ass.) I think I told you that everyone on my list is supposed to have gotten a letter telling them I was coming and why, and that there aren't many telephones so you have to take pot luck, figuring out where everyone lives – Ma Stean is very helpful with that – and trying to get to several people in the same area in one day.

I do it just how Ma told me: I pull up in front of a house, checking with the last name on the mailbox to make sure I'm at the right place, and keeping the bike running. "Halloooo, the house!" I shout, as loud as I can. I've learned the smell of sour mash, which indicates a still somewhere nearby, so I'm particularly careful about those places. I keep the motor of the Indian running because a few times some big hogs have shot out after me and the animals around here mean business.

That's right. I said hogs, not dogs. Except for MacWhirtle, I haven't seen very many pooches around, even out in the country. But I believe these big pigs I've encountered are every bit as threatening as a farm dog, not to mention uglier.

Anyway, when someone comes out and calls off the hogs (if any are around), I turn off the bike and walk up and introduce myself. They are pretty much always glad to see me. They're a lot like the country people we know around Hallock and Northcote, the farmers and such, who don't see many new faces in their lives and are hospitable to the ones they do see.

So they usually ask me in, and I meet anyone else who's at the house (a lot of times they're more shacks than houses). Once we've all talked a little, I get out my tablet and take down the vitals on the person I'm there to interview. It's not uncommon to find another old-timer or two, which means I have a chance of getting more than one story or reminiscence. But sometimes the family members talk over one other and butt into each others' stories and that makes it tough, even though I can keep up pretty good by using that part-shorthand method we worked up all those years ago. Never thought it'd turn out to be helpful in a job, but it is.

The tricky thing is getting the dialect, and then remembering it when I return to Ma Stean's and write up the reports. These folks have a beautiful kind of Southeastern drawl that's hard to get down on paper – like you saw with that witch story I sent you. Sometimes parts of it almost sound like colonial English. I sit and listen and sometimes prompt them with questions like, "Your grandpappy tell you 'bout this more'n once?" I talk as close as I can to how they talk, which seems to be the right way to go about it.

But they know I'm not from around these parts. So they ask me questions, too, and I tell them a little bit about my own grandfather, how he's half-Sioux (although I don't explain that he's nuts and hates Indians), and about the state I come from and all its lakes and how "Minnesota" is Sioux for "cloudy water." They usually want to know about fishing in the state, and I tell them about northern pike, which they don't seem to have around here. We visit for a while and then I leave, either for the next interview or back to Ma's to type up my notes. I don't like for them to get cold. When I lay off too long, as I have a few times, I've been forced to go back to get a point elaborated or clarified, which just puts me behind.

For the most part, these people are dirt-poor, living off the land, although some of them have a family member or two working at the processing plant, which gives them some social and economic standing. All it takes to get in with them is what comes natural, being respectful and remembering the Golden Rule. I get a lot of supper invitations and I rely on my seventh sense, or intuition, or whatever the hell gut feeling I get, to tell me whether to go or not. So far it's worked out fine.

Funny thing, though. Ma has been right with every single name she crossed off my list when I first hit this town. I've tried, but I haven't made contact with a single one of those folks. When I pull up outside their houses and holler the house, nothing happens. Nobody comes out – except, a few times, as I've told you, a pack of half-wild pigs vicious enough to run me off.

So she was right, and she and her friend Mrs. Davis still know a lot of things I don't. I'm sure they know plenty about the cats in this town, and I think that mass grave I found holds more than a few pieces of the Mackaville puzzle. Maybe that's what the old calico was trying to tell me.

And maybe, just maybe, it's all bull shit. If only I could believe that. I wish I could.

Your pal and faithful comrade,

Robert

June 8, 1939, Thursday afternoon

Dear John,

I kinda need to calm down a bunch but I'm really tired and maybe just a tiny tad drunk, too. Don't tell Ma. She "don't 'low it" in her boarding house, liquor I mean, so I'm not sure what to do with the rest of this little jar the boys at the store sent me home with. Thought I might drink it and destroy the evidence. But I've hardly made more than a dent in it and my mind is wandering pretty fierce.

Then I think about what happened today and I snap right back into sobriety. Wish you were right here for me to tell you. I'm going to try to type just like I'm talking to you.

I was out this morning before sunrise. Had three stops I hoped to make way up north and west in the country around a place between mountains the locals call Flat Gap. It was neat driving this road by myself and the sun coming up behind me. Just as I came roaring over a rise I saw a small herd of deer a couple of hundred yards in front of me, leaping and bounding across the road. And then, right behind them, about a half-dozen or so of the ugliest pigs I have ever seen in my life, with black bristly hair and skinny little legs, and I swear they were chasing after the deer. The last pig ran across the road not twenty yards in front of me and just kind of looked casually back as I bore down on him, never breaking stride, like he wasn't afraid at all. I got a glimpse of red eyes and dripping tusks and then I'd zipped past, missing him by only a couple dozen feet.

I mean, these pigs were hideous, evil unnatural spawns of Beelzebub. Well, maybe that's the liquor talking. But I mean they were UGLY, ugly enough to be unsettling. Down the road a little, I pulled off, killed the Indian, and looked back to where they'd crossed, but nothing else came by. I heard a lot of thrashing in the woods. I wondered if they really had been chasing those deer. And if they had, why? I remember hearing that wild hogs would run other animals away from food sources like a wheat or corn field, but these seemed to just be doing it for the hell of it, for meanness maybe. I figured I'd just gotten my first glimpse of Arkansas razorbacks, which a few of my interviewees had mentioned and told me to watch out for when I was up in the hills.

After that encounter with Mother Nature Arkansas style, I got lucky. All three of the people I needed to interview were home and willing to talk, so I finished up a little after noon and stopped at a service station on my way back home to get a little something to eat. That mountain air gives you an appetite.

This place had a couple of old trucks in the drive and four or five locals standing or sitting around a cracker barrel inside, hunkered over a checker game and drinking soda pop. When I walked inside I could tell they thought maybe I was some kind of forest ranger or cop, and given my outfit I couldn't blame 'em. I guess it's about time for me to draw on my big government checks and invest in some work clothes, although I've grown used to my old CCC duds and there's plenty of wear left in 'em.

Anyway, I made kind of a show of introducing myself, telling what I was doing in those parts, and I was so involved in trying to get over as a hail-fellow-well-met kind of guy that I didn't realize it was Old Man Black standing off to one side until I'd stuck my hand out in front of him. You remember – he's the whiskery geezer with the two idiot sons I got into it with on the train platform, the guy Ma Stean called a snake and told me to stay away from.

The old son-of-a-bitch didn't shake my hand. He just glared at me. I shrugged and went over to the pop box, fishing out a Double Cola. I heard him hack and spit behind me, and when I turned around I saw a glob of spittle on the floor, pretty near my boot and nowhere near the cuspidor.

That got me. I doubled up my fist and took a couple of steps toward him, conscious of the other guys in the store watching. I had a foot or so and maybe 50 lbs. on him, but that was too bad.

I was just about to him when he muttered something through those whiskers that sounded like an apology, although I couldn't be sure. It was enough to slow me down, though, and still mumbling, he edged by me and stomped out the door. In just a minute, I heard one of the ancient pick-ups rev up and peel out onto the road.

"Good riddance," said the fat little man behind the counter, who during the introductions had told me his name was Dill Jolley – Dill, like in pickle, he'd said. The others in the store nodded. They were all older guys, none under about 60, in overalls. A couple of them had on straw hats. One or two of them were grinning, and from that evidence it didn't look like there were enough teeth for one good set among the whole group.

"I don't mean to run off your business," I told the proprietor.

"Hell, he never buys nothin' no way."

"Well," I said, "I will. Give me a couple of cans of those sardines and some crackers."

"Help yourself." He nodded toward the barrel where the men congregated. "Some good rat cheese in th' icebox. Three cents fer a big slice."

"Sure. A couple of slices ought to do it."

He picked up a big knife from a butcher-block table behind the cash register, reached down into a little ancient steel Frigidaire, and pulled out what had once been a huge round of cheese. Only about a quarter of it was left, a pie-shaped wedge covered by a coating of red wax. Jolley made a kind of show of cutting off a piece and holding it up.

"Worth three pennies?" he asked.

"You bet."

As he cut off a second slice, I looked around the store. It was what you'd expect out in these hills, nails and tire tubes sharing space with cans of food. The two men who were playing checkers lifted the board up off the top of the barrel, checkers still sitting on it, so I could reach in and get my crackers.

Jolley sacked everything up, I paid him, and he came out from behind the counter and walked to the porch with me, telling me all the while what a horse's arse Old Man Black was. I was just starting to tell him about my encounter with Black's sons when I stepped off the stoop and something whacked me on the left leg, about six inches below my knee.

"Holy hell, boy!" hollered Jolley. "You snakebit!"

By God, he was right. Hanging onto my boot by its fangs was a damned rattlesnake a couple of feet long, writhing and twisting around.

This was one time my theatrical nature paid off. As you know I carry a little sheath knife in the top of my right boot. Well, I dropped the groceries and jerked that knife out, and with one slash of that razor-sharp blade I'd severed that little bastard's head from his body. The body dropped to the ground beside the porch but the head stayed attached, dug into that old stiff CCC leather, God bless it, three layers thick. To think how much I've cussed about how heavy those damn boots are…

I stepped down off the porch, and while that

vile body was twisting around at my feet, covering itself with blood and dust, I stuck the blade squarely between those snake eyes and cut his head right down the middle until it opened into two exact halves, an eye on each one. That killed the son-of-a-bitch, you bet! Then I used the blade to flick off the two pieces.

Jolley's shout had raised the others, and they'd all gathered on the porch to watch the show. I guess they were pretty impressed, because they invited me back into the store, and old Dill dug out a Mason jar full of what he called mountain dew. It was moonshine whisky, sure, and we all had a couple of shots right out of the container. The first one burned all the way down, like I was drinking gasoline. Tasted like it, too. After the second round, I sat down at one of the benches by the cracker barrel and examined my boot to make sure I wasn't really bit. Sure enough, those fangs hadn't gotten through the second layer of leather, much less the third.

These boys made such a to-do over me that I had to sit there and smoke a King Edward cigar with them and knock back another couple of shots. This time, I mixed it with some lime soda pop Jolley offered me and it was pretty damn good. The rest of 'em took it straight, including him.

Well, I had another couple of interviews I wanted to get done this afternoon, but I couldn't very well go to houses smelling like mountain dew, and to tell the truth I'm not all that steady on my feet right now anyway. Ma usually runs her errands on Thursday, so, lucky for me, nobody was around the boarding house but MacWhirtle when I drove the Indian back into the garage. He's sitting here with me now, looking at me like he knows I'm tight. Ma usually doesn't bother me while I'm working, so maybe I'll type up the interviews I did today after I write you. Or maybe I'll just go to bed. Pete's expecting me later, but I'll tell him tomorrow I was sick. Don't want to call him right now. I think the best thing is to quit typing before Ma gets back and knows I'm here. Get a little early shut-eye.

So I'm alive, snockered but alive, a fact I celebrated a little too heartily with my new chums at Jolley's store.

But something's funny. When they took me back in and broke out the 'shine, they were all talking like they thought I was dead for sure, and how I sliced up that rattler, and after the second or third round one of them said, "That'll show old Black." And everybody got quiet for a little bit.

That whiskery old bastard wasn't even there. So what do you suppose he meant? Yeah, I'd better go. It's time to lie down.

Your pal and faithful correspondent,

Robert

June 12, 1939, Monday evening

Dear John,

I'm going to tell you as much as I can with this letter. But there's an awful lot to tell, and if I get pooped I'll have to stop and write more tomorrow. I'll try not to leave you hanging like the end of a Republic serial, but I can't make any promises.

You know from my earlier letters that I've been thinking a lot about that mass grave and what it means, with the cholera epidemic happening exactly 50 years ago. A jubilee? Celebrating the death of maybe a couple hundred people?

I knew that couldn't be right. But I *knew* that grave had something to do with it all.

Finally, I just figured I had to get away and think. At first, I thought about taking Patricia with me, up into the hills that morning, but I nixed that idea. I knew her grandmother wouldn't allow it, for one thing. For another, I didn't know if she'd even go if she could. For a third, I wasn't anywhere near ready to tell her about everything that had been happening, much less how I thought her grandma was somehow involved in it. And lastly, I'd already had someone try to kill or cripple me with a log on one of those roads, and if there was any more danger up there I didn't want her around it.

Mrs. Davis didn't let Patricia go out on

school nights, so I had another date with her set up for Saturday night. I figured if I left early enough I could spend all morning and most of the afternoon in the hills, come back in and help at Pete's service station for an hour or so, and still have plenty of time to pick up Patricia and get to the Mackaville picture show before the newsreel started.

(It's kinda tough, in a good way, to have Patricia there at Ma's every day, helping serve up breakfast and dinner. I try not to flirt or anything. Sometimes I catch her eye and she smiles and kind of blushes, but I don't think any of the other boarders have caught on. Ma knows, of course, but she hasn't said anything to me. Yet.)

So about seven Saturday morning, as soon as the grocery opened, I bought a chunk of ham about the size of a softball (you better like ham if you're going to live in this town), a loaf of bread, and some pickles and apples. I filled up my old CCC canteen, wrapped it and the food in my ground sheet (that's a light tarp for sissy boy townies like you), and tucked it under the seat in my side car beside the sawed-off shotgun and revolver I'd been carrying with me since the log incident. I'd already slipped a few shotgun shells – what was left of the "silver" ones – in my front pants pocket and gotten into that box of Bering cigars your folks gave me last Christmas.

I've really been nursing them. In fact, I haven't had one since I got to Mackaville, because I just want to smoke 'em on special occasions, but this occasion seemed special enough.

With two of those classy smokes resting in my front pocket and everything else in its place, I mounted up on the old Indian in search of adventure, or at least a place to think things over in solitude. It was a beautiful day, and when I stopped in at Pete's Skelly station to gas up and told him what I was doing, he looked really hound-dog envious.

"Why don't you come along?" I said. "You've been telling me for weeks that you'll show me some caves and swimming holes out in the hills. I've got lunch enough for us both, and"—I pulled the two Berings out of my front pocket—"I got smokes that are better than anything you can buy in this burg." Which is true. They don't sell Berings around here – King Edwards and Cremos are about the best you can hope for.

I was just ragging him, so I was surprised when he kinda moved from one foot to another, like he was actually considering it. Then he surprised me again.

"Look," he said. "If Diffie can run the station for me until we get back, I'll do it."

He went inside, and I started checking over the bike. It's a good machine, but it's also a big machine with a lot of little parts to pay attention to. It was down about a half-quart of oil, so I topped her off, and just as I finished Pete walked out with Diffie. Turned out he'd been at the station all along.

"He'll do it," Pete said.

Diffie nodded. "Sure. How ya doin', Robert?"

"Swell," I said, as I tightened up a couple of the fittings on the side car. "Thanks for taking over."

"Glad to." I could see he was a little envious, too.

"It'll be your turn next time," I said.

That seemed to make him happy. He grinned at us as I handed Pete a spare set of goggles.

"All right," I told him. "Let's get outta town."

He adjusted the goggles, leaving them pushed up on his forehead.

"Add this to your plunder," he told me, shoving a handful of candy bars my way. Then, "If you want, I'll drive goin' out, and you can drive coming back. That is if you trust me. I'd like to climb back on her for a little while."

"Sounds good to me," I returned, climbing into the side car. I glanced back at Diffie, whose happy expression had changed to something that looked like bewilderment.

"You gonna fit?" Pete asked.

Folding myself into the side car, I nodded. "Near enough," I told him. My knees stuck out clear above the dash, but I was in. "As long as you stop every once in a while for me to stretch my legs, I'll make it."

Pete nodded, kicked the starter, let that old four-cylinder bang and roar for a few seconds, and we were off. It didn't take him long to get used to my weight and the bike's balance. When he did, he kicked it up to a steady 65 mph, ten miles faster than the limit. I'd be lying if I told you the fact that he'd crashed the Indian twice in the past crossed my mind, but I just let it go and kept an eye out for highway cops. We met one on the way out of town, but Pete slowed in time and waved at the guy as we passed. He waved back. It's a funny thing, but people just seem to look at a motorcycle different, more friendly maybe, when there's a side car attached. Maybe part of the reason is that you don't see many of 'em around.

He headed south and east down through some country I'd never seen, roaring over several miles of macadam through the mountains and then turning off onto a dirt and gravel road that led us to a state highway and a little settlement right where the gravel and pavement met. Three or four stores and a filling station, and a cobbled Main Street that bumped me around pretty good.

"Let's stop and get a Coke," he said above the road of the motor, drifting into the station. "You prob'bly need to stretch anyway."

I groaned in agreement. He grinned.

The guy running the place knew Pete, and they chewed the fat for a little bit, shop talk mostly, while I looked around the place and drank my Coke. It was another Skelly station, pretty much like Pete's, neat enough but not quite as spotless. The location, though, was beautiful, with the walls of mountains rising up all around it. That little town looked like a set of tiny toy buildings at the bottom of a dark-green bowl.

I was checking over the Indian again, not looking for anything in particular, when Pete spoke behind me.

"Hell of a machine," he said.

"You do a hell of a job in the driver's seat," I returned. "Don't want her back, do you?"

"Naw." He took a rag from the pocket of his work uniform – he hadn't bothered to change – and slowly wiped the dust off the headlights. I knew him well enough by now to see that he was making his mind up about something.

"Let's take a walk out back," he said.

"Sure."

Behind the station a lawn studded with engine parts and other automotive stuff went out and gradually sloped upward until it turned into woods. Several big rocks studded the side of the mountain, and we walked to one of those and leaned up against it. This seemed a good time to offer Pete one of my precious Berings. He accepted and we both lit up, smoking in silence for a minute or two. Damn, but those are good cigars!

Finally, Pete blew out a stream of whitish-blue smoke and said, "I ain't been completely honest with you." He gazed up at the mountains, not looking at me.

"That right?"

"'Bout the bike," he added. "I told you I wrecked it twice so I quit riding."

"Yeah."

He turned his eyes on me. "That's true. But I didn't tell you the second wreck killed my wife."

Then he told me the story, just the way Pete tells things, without a lot of emotion or wasted words. It was nobody's fault, really. A truck from the packing house didn't see him and made a left turn just as Pete and his wife got to the intersection at the edge of Mackaville. He was banged up, but she was thrown out of the sidecar onto the road and her injuries were critical. She died a few days later. Pete had insisted on being in the bed next to her, but he was in such bad shape he didn't even know she was gone until the doctor told him a day later. He was doped up with morphine, so it took him a while to understand what was being said, and when he'd pulled himself together enough to look, the bed next to him was empty.

They'd been married 10 months. A baby was on the way.

"So that's how come I never got on that bike again – 'til today," he said. "Knew I had to get back on. Figure you understand now why I was wantin' to drive."

I nodded. "Yeah, Pete. I'm real sorry."

We fell quiet again then, smoking the last of our Berings and inhaling the mountain air, birds chirping and singing in the trees around us. I understood now why Diffie had looked so funny back at the service station, when Pete had asked to drive.

Reluctantly, I dropped the end of the cigar, grinding it into the dirt with my boot. Something told me this was the time.

"Pete," I began, "maybe you can tell me about something else."

He raised an eyebrow.

"When I was cutting up those dimes the other day, to put in shotgun shells?"

"Uh-huh."

"You really didn't want me to do that."

Holding the stub with the tip of his thumb and forefinger, he took one last big drag, letting the smoke curl slowly out of his mouth.

"You don't have to tell me why. I know there's some connection between Mrs. Davis and that cat I was going to shoot. I hope you don't think I'm crazy, but she either has some control over that cat, can see through its eyes or some damn thing, or she _is_ that old calico." I thought about what I'd seen in the cemetery exactly a week earlier, still not entirely sure it hadn't been some kind of apparition.

"You didn't want me to shoot because she and you are friends," I said.

"We're friends, sure," he returned, dropping the remnants of his own cigar to the ground.

"None of that is what I'm asking you – as your friend, too. I'm pretty sure Mrs. Davis was wanting to know if I was reporting to the state about people 'passing for white.' When I showed her I wasn't, she said something about how the town thanked me."

I took a breath.

"Now, I know a lot of the folks in Mackaville and outside in the hills are a little darker than what I'm used to back in Minnesota, where we have all those Scandinavians and Scots, and I'm just wondering, well – does that have anything to do with why Mrs. Davis was so interested in my reports?"

He grinned then. "Might," he said. "C'm'on."

We went back down the hill, I folded myself into the side car, and we were off again, this time off the highway and onto some rougher back roads that jarred my fillings.

"WHERE ARE WE GOING?" I shouted.

"TO MEET SOME RELATIVES OF MINE," he hollered back.

We were way out in the sticks: beautiful green country, but a hard ride. Finally we turned into a neat old farm and out came these folks who, while lighter-skinned, were obviously Negro. Pete watched me while I shook hands and he was obviously pleased with the way I acted around them. Hell, John, I'm no bigot. I've had colored friends before. If that was Pete's family, then that was fine with me. Pete was part-black, he and lots of other people in the town – including Mrs. Davis. I could understand their reluctance to have me report that to the cracker busybody at the state capitol who wrote me that "passing for white" crap. Until I'd talked to Mrs. Davis and Ma, they had no notion whether or not I'd tell on them or not. And if I had – well, Arkansas wasn't the most enlightened state in the union when it came to racial relations.

Pete said as much a couple of hours later, after he took me even further up into the mountains, where we hid the bike in a hawthorn grove and climbed about a half mile to a natural tunnel that went clear through one of the big hills. On the other side was a pocket with a little flat meadow studded with pin oaks and a deep pool of cold spring water, where I had one of the best swims I ever had in my life. Stripping to our skivvies, we stayed in as long as we could stand it – which wasn't long, even with the summer's heat all around us. Pete then showed me a really well-hidden cave on the cliff above the pool, and I made a note to come back and explore it soon. But time was getting away from us and I didn't want to be late for my date with Patricia.

Yeah, I knew that she was colored, or part-Negro, or whatever the hell you want to call it. She had to be because her grandma was. And sure, we've both made jokes about colored people and laughed at Stepin Fetchit and all that. But I'm honestly telling you it didn't make much difference to me where Patricia was concerned.

Our lunch was kind of bass-ackwards, since Pete's relatives had insisted we eat some big old dishes of blackberry cobbler before we left, so we'd had dessert first. Even with that, we polished off everything I'd brought before heading back out. All food's better outdoors, but I hardly tasted anything because I was so intent on listening to Pete's story about why so many people in Mackaville had black ancestors. It had to do, he said, with a Scotsman named MacKenzie who started up the packing plant and the town – Mackaville, makes sense – with the entire cargo of a slave ship back around the 1850s. He hand-picked merchants to come in to take care of the workers' needs, and over the next several years, given the relative isolation of the town and its unusual circumstances, some blacks and whites had begun intermarrying.

MacKenzie was a freethinker, and he didn't mind. And while he kept a pretty tight lid on letting anything get out about the town and its mixed-race population, other Negroes found out about the place and its accommodating nature and several moved there and settled after the War Between the States.

"The folks in Little Rock got their suspicions 'bout us," Pete said. "That's prob'bly why you heard from that fella 'bout all that 'passin' for white' nonsense. But if it ever all really come out, why, no tellin' what'd happen. Klan'd get mixed up in it, most likely. Hell, they might even get the plant shut down, and then there wouldn't be no Mackaville no more."

He fired up a Spud. I passed.

"That's why it was so damn important to Miz

Davis to see if you was tellin' on us. We got to keep things pretty quiet, see."

"I understand, Pete. Thanks for filling me in." I got up, brushing off my pants. "Well, better get back."

"Big date tonight?" He grinned, and I grinned back.

"You bet."

"Don't mind she's colored?"

I shook my head. "I honestly don't," I said.

"Could be trouble, you take her outta Mackaville."

This time I laughed. "I've had one date with her, and you've already got me married. That's a bridge I won't have to cross, at least for a while."

We climbed back down and retrieved the big Indian, and this time I drove. Pete fit in the side car a lot better than I did.

He directed me back to a route I knew from my former trips, and we headed for Mackaville. I had to get back home, change, and make it to Patricia's by about seven, and I knew I'd be cutting it close, so I was gunning the bike pretty good when Pete hollered, "SNAKE!"

I swerved just in time to miss one of the biggest damn rattlers I'd ever seen, stretched out in the road in front of us, head up, tail whirring. Six feet if he was an inch. He actually struck at us as we zipped past.

"DAMN!" I said. Pete was twisted around in the side car, looking back.

I figured it was the sudden appearance of

the snake that spooked me, but I was hit hard then with a cold certainty that something bad was about to happen.

On the next hilltop, I stopped the bike. The late afternoon air was hot, the woods silent. Pete sat up in the side car, looking at me. "Big damn snake," he said.

"You said it."

"Something else wrong?"

"Yeah, but I don't know what," I said. "I've got a feeling." I'd told him a little about my "feelings," so he knew what I meant.

"One of those, huh?"

"Yeah. Wish I knew what it meant. Something's up, though."

"Well, we've only got another five miles or so, and it's all pret' near down hill."

I nodded. "Yeah. Get that shotgun out, will you? And hang on."

As he horsed the shotgun around I let out the clutch and rolled it over the hilltop. I knew the road home, but not like Pete did.

"ANY TURNS AHEAD?" I shouted.

"NAW. GIVE HER HELL!"

So I did. And even with the extra rider and side car that old Indian began to roar. We ripped down the hill, gaining speed with each second. I looked back. A little flame was coming out of the exhaust. We looked like Flash Gordon's rocket ship.

At the same time, my skin felt like ice-cold ants were crawling all over it. I scanned the road ahead for any sign of trouble. For a quick moment, I thought I saw another snake, this time looking at us from the hillside that sped by. Then I thought I saw another. We were going too fast for me to be sure.

We zoomed downward, ever downward, on bouncing and jittering wheels, roaring into a patch of shadow where a mountain blocked out the sun. Then, down the way, I picked up a faint undulation, a silvery line like a spider-web's strand, thicker and bigger –

"GET DOWN PETE! THERE'S A ROPE ACROSS THE ROAD!"

In that second, I heard Pete swear before the shotgun exploded in my right ear. We hit that cable, I ducked, and it flipped off my cap and ripped the shirt right off my back. I hugged the tank as tightly as I could, hoping that Pete was hunkered down in the car, knowing in that instant that if it had been me instead of him in the side car I'd no longer have a head.

Then, I heard him blast again with the shot-gun. Thank God. Swerving and zig-zagging as much as I could, I realized my goggles were gone, too. Pete was firing with my .22 revolver. He emptied eight shots as fast as you can read this. Then we were over a rise and out of their range, whoever <u>they</u> were.

That's when the pain hit me, right across the nose. Blood was blowing into my eyes. I'd been going on adrenaline, but I was shot, maybe bad. John, I sure didn't want to die. I managed to get the bike stopped, turned to make sure

Pete was all right, and passed out right there on the road.

And reliving that is enough for tonight. You know I didn't die, that's the main thing. I'll tell you the rest of the bloody details tomorrow.

Robert, survivor

June 13, 1939, Tuesday afternoon

Dear John,

Sorry to leave you hanging with my last missive. Just ran out of gas. Fact is, I just started working again today, and then only did one interview. But it was a doozy. I'll tell you about it.

First, though, some old business. When last we left Robert, bloody and damn near decapitated, he had staggered off his motorcycle and passed out on the road.

CHAPTER TWO: "HUMAN TARGETS" (Remember how we used to laugh about how every Republic serial had a chapter titled "Human Targets?" I'm here to tell you that being a _real_ human target ain't that damn funny.)

I woke up and thought: _I'm in HELL_! Unbearable lightning-bolt pain blazed through my crotch, my forehead throbbed, wind roared like a tornado past my ears, closed eyes, and drooping head. My arms were pulled back unnaturally, pinned behind me. I had to move, to get the weight off my gonads, which felt like they were being smashed by a rock. But when I tried to shift around and pull myself up, a hand pushed me down again.

"DAMMIT!" I screamed. "STOP THAT SHIT!" Maybe not the best thing to holler in Hell, but if I was there it didn't make any difference what I said anyway.

Instead of Old Nick's laugh, though, I heard

a voice far more welcome, yelling over the roar.

"HELL'S BELLS! YOU'RE ALIVE!" It was Pete, and I felt him grab my shirt and pull me upright.

Although my eyelids seemed to be glued shut, you bet I got 'em open. I saw I was on the motorcycle, sitting in front of him, my private parts jammed up against the gas tank as we blasted toward a setting sun. I squirmed into a little less painful position while Pete cut the engine and slowed us to a stop, jumped off, and grabbed me again. Which was a good thing, because I was about to fall on my face. He held me up and I started stamping my feet, instinctively I guess, restoring circulation, trying to relive the agony below my belt. Webbing was thick in my head, but as he held onto me I heard him say, "I thought you were a dying man, maybe dead already. All I could think about was getting you to a doctor."

I blinked a couple of times, swallowed. "Thanks." I could barely see the sun now. Dusk comes quickly in the mountains. Still, there was enough light for me to see blood, and plenty of it, when I looked down. It was smeared all over my chest and what was left of my shirt, and when I reached up to my cheek some of it stuck to my fingertips. Staring at the sticky red stuff dumbly, like I was in a dream, I barely heard Pete, talking faster than I'd ever heard him talk.

"I didn't know if those sorry bastards were

coming after us or what, so I just pushed you forward, got in the saddle, and took off. I knew I couldn't fold you up enough to fit in the side car," he said, all in one breath. And then, like he was seeing me for the first time, his eyes widened and his hand went to his front pocket, pulling out a rag. He held onto my shoulder with his other hand, keeping me propped up.

"Man, that's where all the blood's coming from!" He jammed the rag above my eyes, looking real concerned. "You got a bullet hole in your forehead!"

I guess maybe I was in shock, because everything seemed to be going very slow, but I knew what he'd said right enough. And now that I thought about it, my head did hurt like hell. I slid my fingers up under the rag, to the source of the pain, and touched something metallic. It was slippery with blood and flesh, but I grasped it and pulled it free. The accompanying wave of agony was enough to make me pass out again, but, feeling Pete's iron grip on my shoulder, I willed myself to stay on my feet.

Without a word, I held the little metal object out, where it caught the glow of the dying sunlight.

"Here," Pete said, guiding my other hand to the rag. "Keep holdin' it to your head." He took the thing from me, examining it.

"Well, I'll be a son-of-a-bitch," he said. He looked at me and actually laughed, the bastard! Here I was bleeding to death, and he thought it was funny?

"You weren't shot at all, you lucky stiff," he said, still grinning. The blood-slicked piece of metal he held up before my eyes was small and square. "Know what this is? It's the buckle for your damn goggles. That rope skinned it off and slammed it into your forehead. A little flesh wound's all you got."

So I wasn't going to die. The news called for something better than a weak grin, but that's all I could muster under the circumstances.

"Think you can ride now?" he asked.

I nodded. Still keeping the rag pressed against my wound, and with him guiding me by the elbow, I managed to fold myself into the sidecar. By this time it was dusk, and about ten minutes later, when we pulled up in front of Pete's Skelly Gas and Tires, night had fallen over Mackaville.

My bones were aching like I had the grippe, but I still managed to pull myself out of the side car – with a little help from Pete – and walk to the building. The lights of the station were on but no customers were around, and Diffie stood in the doorway of the office, waiting. He looked like he was about to needle us about being gone so long, but the grin on his face turned to a look of horror when I came up under the lights.

"Holy moley," he said slowly. "What the hell... ?"

"It's all right," Pete said. "Worse 'n it looks."

I nodded at him and we both walked past Diffie into the office. Sitting down stiffly on the side of the desk, I watched as Pete dug a Coke out of the cooler and handed the wet bottle to me. I still had his rag pressed to my forehead.

"Lemme see," he said, pulling it away. Behind him, Diffie peered in at my wound.

"Bled like a stuck hog," he offered.

"Yeah," agreed Pete. "Get me the first-aid kit, will ya?" Then, to me, "You might wanna wash up 'fore I dress that wound."

I nodded and went back to the big deep sink in the grease-pit bay, washing what blood I could off my hands and arms, and then wetting the oily towel and wiping around my face. There wasn't much I could do for my shirt, which was not only splotched with blood but ripped to tatters by, I guess, the rope across the road.

I'd been damned lucky.

When I returned to the office, Pete and Diffie were there with the kit, and I sat down and let Pete daub my wound with iodine. As far as pain goes, it might as well have been sulphuric acid. When he was all done torturing me, he put gauze over it and bandaged it up, Diffie handing him the stuff he needed with all the efficiency of a nurse in a big-city operating room.

"That'll do for now," Pete said. "Tomorrow's Sunday and the doc's closed, but if it keeps on bleedin' you'd better go see him anyway. He don't mind seein' people if it's an emergency. You may need stitches or somethin'."

"Thanks," I said. I reached in my pocket and threw a nickel on the counter. "How about another Coke before I go?"

I had another, and one more, the sugar and caffeine doing me some good. Or maybe it's that Coca-Cola is a cure-all, like I'm always telling you. Anyway, I sat there until I felt strong enough to leave by myself, and then I went home to Ma's – where I became a human target again, sort of.

I think that's a good place to stop, because I feel like I'd better write up today's interview before it gets cold. I will do my damnedest to give you the whole rest of the story of that crazy night when I write again.

Tell you what. I'll put an extra carbon in the typer when I write up this report, and I'll send a copy in with this letter. I'll have to type hard and hope it's not too light for you to read it, but I think it'll be worth the effort. It's a hell of a yarn, you bet, and since you're always saying how a writer should show things instead of tell things, I'll show you this and see what you think.

I promise to write more tomorrow.

Your friend and faithful correspondent,

Robert

WORKS PROGRESS ADMINISTRATION--FEDERAL WRITERS' PROJECT

Official Form

DATE: 13 June 1939

INTERVIEWER: R.A. Brown

STORY TOLD BY: Mr. Titus Gunnison AGE: 83

ADDRESS: Star Route 1, Mackaville, Arkansas

This here story is about the two Bibles my Grandpa and Grandmama Gunnison uster have.

Papa Jim, we grandkids called him, tole us that he got that extree Bible during the war of the rebellion from a burned-out neighbor of hisn that some bushwhackers had kilt and burnt out. Him and Grammy Mary had them that extree Good Book for some thuty years afore they had need of it.

Papa Jim weren't shy about tellin' us youn-guns all 'bout it, 'specially of a night we was wantin' a scary story. He'd gather us all 'round and look usn's over, and then he'd start right in. Here's as I remember it:

One night in the dark of the moon, Papa Jim's old dawg woke him up with howlin' and carryin' on, and didn't take Papa Jim long to know somethin' had th' chickens in th' hen house upset. He'd been losin' some birds right regular, so up he jumps in his night shirt, pulls on his boots, and a-grabbin' his shotgun and lightin' a kerosene lantern, he hotfoots it outside. He could hear them chickens carryin' on a-squawkin', and when he opened the hen house door, he sees thar in th' yeller light of th' lantern the biggest ole rattle snake he'd ever come across. Up comes the shotgun and he blowed that snake right in haff, leavin' them two parts a-wigglin' on th' floor.

Then ole Papa Jim, he jest shuts up th' door and goes back to bed, figgerin' them chickens'd pick apart them old snake halves right down to the bone 'fore mornin'.

But thet ain't what happened. And right about here in th' story he'd narrer his eyes and get his voice way down deep an' growly. No sir, he'd say, what he'd shot was still layin' there in the morning. Them chickens was huddled in a corner of th' coop, fur away from it as they could get.

So Papa Jim goes out to th' pasture jest back of the big barn and starts to dig him a big ole deep hole fer buryin'. He wanted it seven foot deep he tole us, 'cause eight foot is for Bible-believin' Christians and even injuns but not for no snakes.

While he was a-diggin' two more big rattlers snuck up and tried to bite him but he seen 'em comin' and chopped 'em up good with his shovel. Havin' two of 'em sneak up on him like that kinda got him to thinkin', so after he drug that body out of the hen house and dropped it in the grave hole, he dropped in the bodies of the two snakes he'd kilt that mornin' and then went in and got that extry Bible and put it thar on top of them dead rattlers. Then he filled that hole up. After that, they never had no trouble with no rattlers ever again, nor with chickens bein' kilt or disappearin', 'ceptin' for a coyote getting' one every oncet in a while.

They was some little disturbance pret' near all over the county for a time after that, 'bout a fella who'd disappeared without no trace. The sheriff even came to visit once. But Papa Jim jest kept his mouth shet and it all finely blowed over.

He'd end up his tale by tellin' us younguns how Caleb Black was no damn good anyway, a chicken thief and prob'bly a lot worse. Yep, he said, he'd been surprised to see old Caleb's body blowed near in haff and layin' there on the hen house floor when he'd checked that mornin', but Papa Jim knew he'd shot a snake the night before, and he knew thet extry Bible ud keep it buried, whether man nor beast, fer good and all.

June 14, 1939, Wednesday night

Dear John,

Full day of interviews today and I'm beat, but I promised I'd finish telling you the tale of that fateful Saturday, so here goes:

I didn't want anyone at Ma's to see me in the shape I was in – especially Ma herself – so I cut the engine on the old Indian a couple of blocks from the boarding house and pushed it the rest of the way. That took some muscle, and I still wasn't in very good shape, so I had to stop and rest a few times and still almost passed out a time or two before I got it into the garage.

As it turned out, I could've saved myself that effort. The house was dark when I got there, not a boarder nor Ma in sight. So I got everything out of the bike, my sawed-off shotgun and pistol and water bottle and a couple of candy bars left from our trip, shook out the ground sheet, and draped it over the Indian. There was moisture in the air and maybe even rain – I glimpsed some lightning up in the hills to the east – and that old shed was not any too waterproof.

When all that was done, I gathered up my stuff, let myself in the back door with my key, and went into the kitchen. Ma had told me that if I ever came in hungry and she wasn't around I could help myself to what was in her ice box, and I hoped she was as good as her word because I suddenly felt starved. Leaving everything on the sideboard, I got the pitcher of ice water out, poured a big tumbler full, and then saw the leftover meatloaf we'd had a couple of nights before. My head started to spin when I reached in to get it; I hadn't realized how weak I still was. But I recovered in a minute and sat down to my cold dinner.

I'd taken exactly one big bite when I heard a skittering of claws in the hall, followed by the sudden appearance of my pal MacWhirtle, galloping ninety to nothing and skidding to a stop right at my feet. Sure, he's a chow hound and can probably hear an ice box door opening in the next county, but I think he was just as concerned about me as he was about the meat loaf he knew I'd share. Even after it was gone, he kept licking my hands and whining. I wondered if he knew what my torn and bloody shirt and forehead bandage meant. I do know that he insisted on climbing into my lap, where he sat, looking up at me with what I could swear was real concern.

I petted him for a minute or two, then I started worrying about the questions I'd have to answer if anyone came home and saw me looking like I did.

"C'm'on," I told MacWhirtle, letting him down to the floor as I got up. "We'd better blow this pop stand before someone sees me." I rinsed off my plate and glass, put them in the dish drainer and, picking up my weaponry and water bottle, headed upstairs, my little buddy at my heels.

Although I was sure no one was around, I went up the stairs as quietly as I could, remembering what we'd learned as kids about walking next to the wall so that the steps didn't creak and give you away.

My door was closed and locked, as usual, so I used my other key and stepped aside to let MacWhirtle go in first.

But he stopped dead, eyes wide, every hair on his little body suddenly standing up. His lips pulled back into a snarl. He was trembling all over, making a noise like an electric shaver.

Well, I was just tired enough of this shit. I reached in my pants pocket and felt for a couple of shotgun shells – the ones with the cut-up dimes I'd pocketed earlier. Levering open the sawed-off Stevens, I shoved 'em in and got down into a slight crouch, ready to shoot.

"Get back, Mac," I whispered. "Back." I had to skootch his stiff little body back, out of the line of fire, with my foot. He acted like he didn't even know he was moving, still on point, still growling low in his throat. A courageous dog, MacWhirtle.

I peered into the room, trying to spot the source of his concern. The light from the hall's 25-watt bulb is pretty dim, so I reached through the doorway and flipped the wall switch.

John, it took all the guts I've got and then some to do that. It was like that time when you and I were kids, in your kitchen, and your mom had eggs boiling on the stove. Remember?

She'd gone out of the room for a minute, and I told you that I could stick my hand in boiling water and not get burnt. When you expressed skepticism, I turned on the tap in the sink, held my hand under the cold water for a couple of seconds, and then, with a nonchalance I didn't really feel, I plunged my hand in the pan and came up with an egg. I enjoyed the effect it had on you – for about one second, and then I let go of that egg with a holler. The water hadn't burned me, sure enough, but that eggshell had blistered my fingertips.

Sticking my hand in that room felt just like shoving it into that pan full of boiling water – and I guess I expected the equivalent of a burning hot egg.

It didn't happen. I stood there with Mac between my feet, still "rrrrrring" away, so agitated he was almost standing on his toes, peering hard into a familiar room that had suddenly turned sinister. The bedclothes looked a little mussed; I was sure I hadn't left them that way. But as hard as I looked, I couldn't see anything else out of place. I was screwing up my courage to step in when a sudden gust of wind outside brought a spray of rain against the window – and the screen moved.

That's when I figured it out. The window

screen had only moved in and out a tiny bit, but it was enough to tell me it had been unlatched. And I hadn't done it. I never unlatched the screen.

I don't mean to get all nostalgic again, but you remember how you and I figured out how to use a piece of wire to unlatch your bedroom window so we could sneak in after being out too late? I knew in a moment that someone had gotten up on the roof and done just that.

Leaving the light burning, I stepped back, pushed the door shut, and locked it. Turning the key in the lock, I found the stub of a pencil in my shirt pocket and jammed it in under the key.

Whoever or <u>whatever</u> was in there would play hell coming through that door. It would have to be broken down.

I glanced up quickly. I'd forgotten about the transom, the one the old calico had jumped through. Luckily, it was closed.

"Come on, Mac," I said. "Other quarters for us tonight."

I reached down and scooped him up with one arm, holding the shotgun in my other hand, noticing for the first time that I seemed to be shaking a little bit. Hate to admit it, but I guess you can hardly blame me. Old Mac kept staring daggers back at the door as we slipped down the hall. I was going to say "tip-toed," but we both know that if you want to move quietly you walk on the outside edges of your feet, staying balanced, testing each step before putting your full weight down. I was moving like that, although I couldn't tell you why. Rain had started drumming on the roof, blown by the wind and making far more noise than we were.

I guess I was going on pure adrenaline for the second or third time in a few hours, and when I got to the bathroom at the end of the hall and switched on the light, letting Mac to the floor, an immense tiredness swept over me. After shutting the door, I almost tumbled to the floor, plopping instead down on the commode. I sat there for I don't know how long, lightheaded, trying to get my breathing back to normal, watching Mac's fur slowly relax. He sat there, his eyes on me, ready for anything.

I knew what I was ready for. I had to get some sort of rest. Just close my eyes.

Maybe I still wasn't thinking too straight. I did consider making a call to the sheriff's office, but what would I tell him? I had an idea what was in my room, a premonition I guess, but I didn't know for sure, and it could just as easily have been gone by the time he got here. Hell, if whatever it was heard me, it might creep out the window and nail me while I was on the phone. Besides that, I'd have to explain my appearance to a lawman who didn't seem to like me much anyway, and that would open up a whole new can of worms.

Plus, I wasn't too crazy about leaving the relative security of the bathroom right away.

So I sat there, eyes closed, trying to plan

a course of action. After several minutes, I got up and opened the linen closet. Pulling out all the towels, I laid them in the bottom of that big old cast-iron, claw-footed bath tub. Then I took the community towel off its nail, soaked it under the tap in the sink, wrung it out, and tamped it into the space at the bottom of the bathroom door.

That would have to do.

The only window in the bathroom was closed and latched and there was no transom, so our little fort was as secure as I could make it.

I've slept in bath tubs before and they are not built for someone my height, but they're better than a floor, especially a floor in a house with some sort of horror creeping around in it. So I eased myself down and pulled one of the towels up for a makeshift pillow. Without any coaxing, Mac climbed in, and with him and the shotgun for company, I settled in and felt sleep pull me down like quicksand.

Then, the scream.

It ripped through my consciousness like chain lightning. I'd never heard Patricia scream before, so don't ask me how I knew it was her. I just _knew_.

I grabbed my shotgun and was getting to my feet before I even opened my eyes. Right beside me, MacWhirtle barked like a tommy gun.

"_Hold_ it, son!" came a hard voice, one that I knew.

My eyes were sticky again, but I got 'em

open. The grizzled face of Sheriff Meagan stared back at me, his hand on the butt of the Remington .44 he'd shot into the air the night the Black boys had braced me at the train depot. I looked down, saw I had the shotgun pointed squarely at him.

"Sorry," I muttered, lowering the barrel. Over his shoulder, I saw Patricia, her eyes wide with horror, hand to her mouth, staring at me. Next to her was her grandmother and Ma Stean, and Mister by-God Clark, arms hanging down at his sides like a gorilla's, mouth gaping. They all looked like they expected me to jump out of the bath tub and chase 'em around the room.

Except for the sheriff. He just looked pissed off.

"Better just go ahead and set her down," he said, nodding at my sawed-off weapon. I nodded back and placed it gently on the towels beneath me in the tub.

Something was in my eyes. I brushed at it with one hand. The fingers came away sticky and red.

Mac had stopped barking, so it was real quiet in that bathroom. So quiet that I heard Patricia's sharp intake of breath when I looked at my fingers. It's funny. I was maybe bleeding to death, a sheriff was threatening to plug me, and in the middle of it all I suddenly remembered that Patricia and I were supposed to be at the movies that night. I'd stood her up.

I tried to smile like Errol Flynn, kinda crooked. Looking at her, I said, "If we hurry, we might be able to catch the second feature." I had no idea what time it was. It just seemed important that she knew I remembered we had a date.

She swallowed and tried to smile back. The sheriff interrupted our moment by telling me, "You know you've scared the bejeebers outta these folks. They thought someone shot you and dumped your carcass in the tub."

What had happened was that Mr. Clark had gotten off his regular Saturday shift and stopped at the Green Hog to hoist a few before returning home. When he got in, half-shot I bet, he quite naturally had to drain his radiator, and when he opened the door to the bathroom, there I was, a sight right out of the true-detective magazines. My error had been in forgetting to lock the door when Mac and I had forted up for the night. Mr. Clark, figuring me for a stiff, had called the sheriff. Just after he arrived, Ma Stean returned from visiting her pal Mrs. Davis. She'd planned to be over at the Davis house when I came to pick Patricia up, maybe to needle me a little; when I hadn't shown, all three of them had come over to the boarding house, worried that something might have happened. (This just gives further credence to the idea that there's something going on here, something maybe murderous, that's still beyond my understanding, if not my sensing.) When they found the sheriff's car outside, they ran upstairs and found him and Mr. Clark – and me.

I found all that out later. There in the bathroom that night, I had more immediate concerns. I touched my hand to the bandage Pete had put on. It was wet and tacky, and I knew whatever Pete had done hadn't been enough to stanch the bleeding.

"What happened to you?" Sheriff Meagan asked.

"I had a wreck on my motorcycle and drove the buckle of my goggles into my forehead," I said, touching the bandage again. "When I got back I was a little woozy. Thought I might throw up, so I laid down in the tub so I'd be close to the toilet and not get sick on Ma's floor." It was mostly a lie, of course, but it came out sounding pretty natural.

"Who patched you up?"

"Pete Barlow, over at the Skelly station." I touched the wet gauze again.

"Well, he's a good mechanic but he ain't no doctor," the sheriff said. "Lemme go call the real doc, see if he's still up. You might need stitches."

"All right." I nodded, and it hurt. I really wanted to lie back down again, but thought it best to stay on my feet. I gingerly stepped out of the tub onto the well-worn linoleum floor.

"You feelin' okay now?" It was Ma, looking worried.

"Yes ma'am," I said. "More or less."

I heard the water in the sink running, and

Patricia came up, washcloth in hand. "Here," she said. "You look terrible."

"Well, you look great."

She turned her eyes shyly away. "Tell me if it hurts," she said, rubbing around the bandage gently with the damp cloth. It did, a little, but I took it. She smelled wonderful, like Lifebuoy and lavender all mixed together. I was being tended to by an angel, and I didn't want it to stop.

"God bless you," I whispered, and she blushed.

Sheriff Meagan was the killjoy. As Patricia ministered to me, Ma Stean stabilizing my head with her big hands with Mrs. Davis and Mr. Clark looking on solicitously, he shouldered his way back into the bathroom and said, "Doc's home and waitin'. Let's go."

Taking me by a shoulder, he guided me toward the door, with maybe a little more force than was necessary.

"May I go along?" Patricia asked.

"Sorry," he said, looking back as he continued to guide me out. "I've got a few questions for Mr. Brown that might get kinda confidential. He'll be safe enough with me."

She nodded, and I gave her a little wave, even though I wasn't feeling all that jaunty. In fact, the jolt of adrenaline – I was surprised I had any left – that had hit me upon awakening was fading fast, and I was getting all light-headed again.

We marched down the stairs and out into a

night left humid by the passing rain. The sheriff opened the passenger-side door for me and as I started to get in, he said, "Just a damn minute!"

It scared me stiff. Now that we were away from everyone, was he going to lower the boom?

"Turn around," he said, producing a pocket flash and running the beam over me. After a few moments, he snicked the light off.

"Guess there ain't no wet blood on your back, is there? Or your butt?"

"Nossir," I said. "Don't think so."

"All right. Be careful." He helped ease me through the door. "I don't want no blood stains on my seat covers. Hard as hell to get out."

I felt better after that, but I still didn't know how much I could tell him about what had happened without getting my ass into an even bigger crack. On the other hand, I didn't want to just flat-out lie to him. So when he asked me to tell him everything that had happened, I decided on the spot to be truthful as possible but to keep my suspicions to myself. That included the suspicions about what was in my room. I just hoped Ma wouldn't open it up before I got back.

I explained how Pete and I had been on an outing in the mountains and, coming back, had been shot at, returned fire, and hit a rope.

"Where'd it happen?" he asked.

I told him the location as best I could, using the names of people I'd interviewed in the area as markers. "Maybe they thought we were federal agents," I said. "Revenuers."

"Old Man Black and his boys live out that way," he said, and as soon as he did I knew it was them. I knew it.

"That right?" I returned.

"I remember you had a little dust-up with 'em the night you came to town."

"Yessir."

"Any way they would've known you were out there? In time to set up an ambush, I mean."

And John, it was like a movie in my head. I saw once again that big damn snake in the road, saw, or felt, others that had been watching us from the woods, and I knew somehow they were connected sure as hell to Old Man Black and his oaf sons, just like that rattler that had attacked me at Jolley's Mercantile. First cats, now snakes. In a flash, I was sure it all fit together.

"Naw," I said, not eager to share my sudden seventh-sense insights with him. "I don't see how."

"You wouldn't have been out there prowlin' around, lookin' for 'em?"

"Nossir." I figured we ought to be at the doctor's about now. Mackaville wasn't *that* big of a town.

As if he'd read my thoughts, the sheriff said, "Since you don't look or sound like you're gonna die real soon, we'll take the scenic route to Doc Chavez's, drive around a little."

I didn't like the sound of that, but I nodded anyway. My head still throbbed like hell. "You're aware that under the National Firearms Act of 1934, it's illegal for you to own a shotgun with a barrel length of under 18 inches. I didn't take a tape measure to it back there, but I'm bettin' yours ain't that long." He said it conversationally, like he was asking me about the folks back home.

"Actually, sheriff, I've measured it," I said. "It's a good eighth of an inch over the legal minimum."

"You were just real careful, weren't you?" he returned, hardness creeping into his voice.

"I was. The only reason I cut it down is so it'd fit in the sidecar of the motorcycle I'm renting from Pete."

He looked over at me. "What kinda loads you got in that ol' Remington?"

That was a damn smart question. It told me he still had an idea that I'd gone out gunning for Tweedledum and Tweedledee Black. If I'd told him "deer loads," he'd know those could kill a man and that might've been my purpose. Bird shot, on the other hand, could inflict some pain, but if you knew anything about weapons you wouldn't try to murder someone with it.

"Number eights. We were thinking we might see some dove, maybe quail." This came out fast and natural, because it was mostly true. That's the kind of shells he'd find if he looked in the shotgun. I'd just modified 'em a little with those cut-up dimes.

"Outta season."

"Yessir." I tried to look penitent. "But we didn't get any anyway."

He didn't say anything to that. We drove through the dark streets a couple of minutes in silence, and then he slowed to a stop in front of an old two-story set back behind a picket fence. He nodded toward it.

"Doc's place," he said.

"Thanks." I started to get out, but he clasped his hand on my nearest shoulder, stopping me.

"Brown," he began. "You seem all right, but you wear them CCC clothes and walk around all buzzed up like you know something none of the rest of us do. People 'round here got the idea you know more'n you let on."

He paused, his hand still on my shoulder. The light from a lamp down the street threw a dim halo around his head.

"My family's only been in this town a couple generations. Ma and Pa come in back around the turn of the century to run a little general store. Mr. MacKenzie was alive then and still runnin' things. He hand-picked my folks for th' job – like he did all the merchants."

That sounded like something I'd like to know more about. But I knew this wasn't the time to be playing Twenty Questions.

"Most of the families 'round here go a lot farther back, and they know stuff I'll never know," he continued. "They're clannish — and there's more'n one clan, too. I might be wastin' my breath. You may not have no idea what I'm talkin' about. But for all that struttin' around you do, pokin' your nose around, you seem to be a pretty intelligent fella. So I'm suggestin' somethin' to ya."

"All right, sheriff," I said.

"This is where I live, an' I'll be here the rest of my life. You're gonna be outta here in a few weeks or months or whenever. I've learned to live with th' mysteries around this place. To leave 'em alone an' go on about my business. You might oughtta try the same thing. Stop actin' like Black Jack Pershing, diggin' up an' bullin' your way through stuff. Walk a little softer. Be a little less... curious. Understand?"

My fingers went once again to the bandage on my head. "Yessir," I said again.

"Just advice. That's all." He nodded toward the house. "Doc's waitin'." Reaching across me and popping the passenger-side door open, he got out on his side and walked with me up to the house. The porch light was on, and when he knocked I glanced over at him and realized that he didn't look like most of the people I'd seen in Mackaville, sure enough. His broad face was ruddy, but he was as pale-skinned as I was.

Well, I told you I'd give you the whole shebang in one helping, but I'm looking back on all the sheets I've typed and enough is enough. There's more to tell for sure. So you'll get another letter from me in a day or two. Hell, something new might have happened by then anyway.

Your long-winded pal and faithful correspondent,

Robert

P.S. I have a big favor to ask. Will you drive up to my house and get a couple of my books on magic? There's one I have on were-animals titled <u>The Human Animal</u>. Also one called <u>The Book of Black Magic</u>, and another, <u>Magic in the Islands</u>. I could also use that two-volume set, the real old one, called <u>An Examine of Witch Craft and Spells</u> all about witches in the colonies and how they worked. You remember that one, I bet. We found it in that old bookstore in Minneapolis, and I talked you into lending me all of fifty bucks so I could get it. They're all right there on the same shelf as my <u>Weird Tales</u> collection, at either end.

You can tell Mom or Dad that I sent you to get 'em, but don't say any more than that. I haven't been telling them anything about what's going on in this town, so keep all that to yourself. They hear too much and they might want to send me to the laughing academy in Faribault, like they did Grandmother. I know she really was nuts there at the end, but they might think the same thing about me if they knew half the stuff I've been telling you.

Anyway, please get those books at your first opportunity and send them first-class. I know it'll cost over a buck, and more than that, I know you have to drive to Hallock, so I'm enclosing a fiver with this letter. Pay for your gas and the postage and keep the rest of it. It's damned important for me to get those books as quick as I can. It really could be a matter of life and death.

June 15, 1939, Thursday night

Dear John,

I can only imagine what you think about this latest escapade of mine. The last letter I got from you is the one where you talked about the mass grave and the snake at Jolley's and all that other stuff that now seems like a distant memory, displaced by this new set of circumstances I've written you about in my past three letters. Four, counting this one. Not that I don't think about those other things. I'm just up against more urgent stuff now, which is why I wrote you about sending those books.

I've thought about telephoning you and catching you up all at once. It's not the long-distance cost that keeps me from it. I want to have all this down on paper in case something happens to me. A record of what I've done and seen. This just seems like the best way to do it, sending it all to a pal I trust above everybody else.

The doc, Dr. Chavez, was a little guy, past middle age but robust, built like a beer barrel and coffee-and-cream colored like most of the rest of the folks in Mackaville. The "Chavez" indicated there might be a little Mex in him; I don't know. He was real efficient, though, and didn't seem at all disturbed about having to work after his normal hours. He let us in, saying hi to the sheriff like old pals do and ushering me into this room he'd made into a little home office.

Patricia had done a pretty good job of wiping the blood off my face, but there was some new seepage, and he took care of that and then pulled the old bandage off. It didn't hurt as much as I thought it would. I guess the blood had weakened the adhesive.

He poked around on my forehead a little, "hmming" to himself, and that did hurt. He swabbed at it, put some stuff on it, and told me I needed a couple of stitches.

I braced myself. But I wasn't prepared for what came next.

"I guess you're the fella shot the Black twin," he said as he worked on me. I almost flinched.

"Picked some shot out of his arm a couple hours ago," he added. "Hold still, now. Number eight shot, looked like, and a couple little silver pieces. You got the better end of it, I'd say."

Hoping the sheriff wasn't paying too much attention – I didn't even know if he was in the room – I said, "Pete, my friend Pete, shot him. Somebody opened up on us while we were out riding on his motorbike. Pete returned fire. I didn't know it was one of the Blacks."

That was kind of a lie. I'd known it as soon as the sheriff said the Blacks lived out that way. I might've even known it before that.

The doc finished sewing and stepped back

before speaking again. "Yeah," he said. "That looks all right. You might live after all."

He grinned then and applied a fresh dressing. Then he gave me some gauze and tape, a tube of sulfa drug to put on the wound, and a couple of headache pills, telling me to change the bandage every couple of days and come see him at his downtown office in about a week — quicker if the skin around the catgut got puffy or started bleeding again.

I'd been sitting on a long examination table, and when I got up I saw to my relief that Sheriff Meagan was nowhere around. I'd hoped he hadn't been eavesdropping when Doc Chavez brought up the silver mixed in with the shot he'd dug out of the Black twin.

"That'll be three dollars," said the doc. "And I'm throwing in something else."

He turned to a medical cabinet in the wall just about level with his head, reached in and pulled something out as I dug three singles out of my wallet. It was a large, red, rubber capsule, a little bigger than a 12-gauge shell.

"A snakebite kit," he said. "You got one?"

"Nossir. No, I don't." I took it from him. "How much I owe you?"

He chuckled. "Nothing. My gift. Anyone kicks one of the Blacks in the butt has my support." His grin left. "I've got anti-venom, too, here and at my office downtown. Remember that." He nodded toward the old monitor-top refrigerator over in the corner.

"I'll remember," I said. "Thanks."

"Old man Black is crazy, and his sons are none too sane," he said, opening the office door for me. "You'll want to watch out."

I said I'd do that.

The trip back to Ma's was uneventful. Apparently Sheriff Meagan had said all he wanted to say to me. Just before he dropped me off, I thought again about telling him about the window and my room and what I thought was in there. But what if I was wrong? You know better than anybody that every once in a while my seventh sense turns out not to be a seventh sense at all, but maybe just imagination or wishing something was so. Like when Tige went missing back when we were both in junior high, and I was sure he'd gotten lost chasing something and was running around outside of town. I even thought I was being guided to where he was by my "powers."

You know how that turned out. I got Dad to drive us over every farm-to-market road in rural Hallock, and when we got back Mom told me he'd been run over and killed the next block over. It wasn't the seventh sense. I just wanted him to still be alive.

There was a chance this was the same thing, although in this case I wanted the something in my room dead, not alive. Or better still, not there at all. So I said nothing to the sheriff except thanks for the ride, and as soon as he'd left, I headed out to Ma's garage. I had an idea, and this time it wouldn't involve shooting up her boarding house.

I was hoping I had enough left after all the events of the evening to do this one last thing.

So I uncovered the big Indian and once again pushed it along for a couple of blocks. When I thought I was far enough away from Ma's, I fired it up and headed for Pete's house.

He lived in a little bungalow within walking distance of the Skelly station. Even though my strap watch told me it was nearly 11 p.m., there was a light on when I pulled up. Through the front window I saw him sitting in a rocker in his neat little living room, reading a copy of Liberty magazine.

If he was surprised to see me, he didn't show it. He answered my knock, looked me up and down, and said, "Ain't had time to change clothes, I see."

"No. Been to the doc."

He studied my bandage in the glow of his porch light. "Hmm," he said. "C'm'on in."

"Not right now, thanks. I'm wondering if I could borrow those two fire extinguishers you've got at the station."

"Sure, I guess." He reached down to a little table just inside the door for a key ring, which he handed to me.

"They're carbon tet, aren't they?"

"Yeah. Where's the fire?"

I grinned, and when I told him why I wanted 'em, he looked at me sideways. "Well, I guess it oughtta work," he said finally. "If that's really whatcha got."

"If it is, I'll buy you a couple of replacements," I told him. "Thanks."

I took the chance of riding into Ma's garage after I picked up the two brass extinguishers, figuring everyone ought to be in bed and asleep now that they figured the excitement was over. I didn't see the Chevy roadster in the driveway, so Patricia and Mrs. Davis had gone on home, too. I was glad about that, especially if my suspicions were right about my room. No sense in putting anyone else in danger.

Lugging the two metal bottles up the stairs, trying not to clink them together and make noise, I got ready for war. First, I crept down to Dave's room. He'd been on the midnight shift up at the depot for a couple of weeks, so I knew his room was unoccupied. It wasn't locked, either, and I went in and borrowed a straight-backed chair, bringing it back down to my own door. Then I pulled my sheath knife out of my boot and its leather case, using it to dig the pencil lead out of the lock. I kept it handy.

Now came the tricky part. I didn't want to wake anybody up, but I needed to make a little noise. So I took a chance and stamped my foot several times hard on the floor just outside the door, shaking the knob at the same time.

I exhaled, steeling myself. This was it.

I turned the key in the lock and cracked open the door, knife in hand. Nothing.

Another inch, and the coast was still clear. I opened it wide. No sign of anything. A little wind came up and lifted the window screen for a moment. That was all. Climbing up on the chair, I opened the transom all the way. Then I climbed down, set the knife on the chair's seat, and backed up, gently pushing the door until it was open just enough for me to stick the nozzle of the fire extinguisher through.

I opened her up, shooting a pencil-thick stream of carbon tet under my bed. It fizzed like it was going to explode and maybe it did because all of a sudden a huge rattlesnake blew out like a rocket from beneath the bed – not slithering but airborne and headed right for me! I slammed the door shut, heard the body wham against the wood.

Jumping up on the chair, I stuck the nozzle through the open transom and sprayed that baby but good, emptying one extinguisher and replacing it with the fresh one. I knew by this time the noise was probably waking up everyone in the house but I couldn't help it, couldn't stop now. Carbon tet is heavier than air, so I knew it was displacing the oxygen on the floor and forcing that damn thing to breathe in those vapors. I peered through the transom then, and saw four feet of reptile rolling around under that steady stream of carbon tet, thrashing and lifting its hideous head, stretching its jaws open so the twin fangs showed white and glistening. I sprayed until the stream from the second extinguisher died. By that time, the snake wasn't moving much. I pulled aside the chair, grabbed up my knife, jerked the door open, and hacked that son-of-a-bitch into about fifty bloody pieces. I know it was fury at being scared so, but there was also a kind of triumph in it. I knew I had a snake in my room. My seventh sense told me. That's why I'd stamped my foot and rattled the doorknob. You and I both know that snakes hear through vibrations, so by warning it I was coming I gave it a chance either to come out after me in full view or hide and wait – and since the only place something as big as that can hide in that room is under my bed, it gave me time to set my plan into action.

After I'd chopped that snake into hamburger, I opened up the window and turned the fan on high, searching every inch of my room in case there were any other surprises. Carbon tet has a strong smell and I got a little light headed, so I shut the door and went out into the hall, sitting down on Dave's straight-backed chair.

I heard footsteps and muttered voices. Once again, Robert had shaken up the household.

Ma was the first to reach me, an old robe thrown around her, her salt-and-pepper hair tangled atop her head. Mac was right with her, scrambling to stay up.

"Land sakes, Mr. Robert Brown," she said. "What is it this time?"

I nodded toward my opened door. She peered in.

"Sweet baby Jesus in Heaven," she said quietly. Mac stood at the door sill, peering in. He wasn't all puffed up again, but he didn't show any inclination to enter the room, either. He kept looking into it, and then back to me.

Somewhere around that time, tall Paul in pajamas and stocky Mr. Clark in undershirt, shorts, and a ratty bathrobe, looking like Mutt and Jeff, appeared and stood at the doorway to my room with Ma, gazing in at the carnage and talking in low tones. I just sat there, used up, the smell of carbon tet still hot in my nostrils, thinking about how it had been one hell of a day.

Your pal and faithful correspondent,

Robert

June 21, 1939, Wednesday night

Dear John,

Man, you didn't let any grass grow under your feet! You must've driven up to my folks' house, picked up the books I asked for, and sent 'em out all the same day you got my letter. You didn't say so, but I imagine you mailed them from the Hallock p.o. before driving back, which probably got them to me 24 hours quicker. I hope you didn't have to take off work to do all that, but I'll bet you did.

Anyway, they arrived Monday – via Air Mail! I figured you'd be able to promote a couple of lunches and a beer or two at the Press Club with the change from that five-spot I sent you.

Instead, you used most of it to get the books here quicker. A true pal. Thanks.

I'm glad that story I sent you about the snake/person in the hen house gave you the shivers. Maybe a couple of months ago I would've just seen it as a tall hill-billy tale myself. Now, though, I wouldn't be a bit surprised if it really happened.

To tell you the truth, I'm not sure _what_ could surprise me now. I've been wondering how I've started accepting as fact things that rightfully belong in _Weird Tales_. Fiction. Except it's not.

Accepting the idea that those cats were staring at me from the bone yard the night I rode into Mackaville was the way it began.

Then, as the other stuff I've been telling you about started happening, and things began getting stranger and stranger, it got easier for me to buy into the whole scene, to believe that some of the cats I'd seen and people I'd met had some sort of eldritch bond. Then came the snakes, which make the cats seem as benign as my old Aunt Nellie.

After only six weeks in this crazy little burg, I feel like I'm living my days in a different reality, separated from my old life not only by miles but by the whole idea of what "normal" is. Some of the stories I've gotten, like the two I've sent you, just reinforce that feeling.

I think maybe my whole life I've been preparing for this. It's not just having the seventh sense since I was a kid, although that's a big part of it. It also has to do with how I've always skirted the edges of messing with black magic – lots of times with you. Remember how we planned to filch a couple of stethoscopes from Dr. Jennings' office and go out to the grave yard at night to see if we could hear dead people breathing? We planned a lot of that sort of stuff, even though I was too chicken to go through with most of it. You didn't know that. I always let you back out first, then ridiculed you. Or maybe you did know it and didn't say anything.

Anyway, not to be melodramatic, I'm thinking what's happening here is something I was destined for. I know, like the sheriff said, I won't be here forever and it might be best just to keep my nose clean and not turn over any more rocks. But it could be too late to turn away now. It's obvious that people are trying to kill me. But I'm pretty sure they constitute a very small part of this town's population. It may just be three people, in fact: Old Man Black and his twin idiot offspring.

After the books came yesterday, I took several hours when I should've been transcribing interviews and studied up on a few things. Going on that, my sense about what's happening, and some of the things people I trust like Ma and Pete and Mrs. Davis have told me, I've come up with the idea that a lot of the folks around here, especially the old-timers, have a spiritual or magical or whatever you want to call it "link" to certain animals. One of the books you sent me suggests that people like this can <u>become</u> those animals, but I don't think this is the case here — even though I still have my questions about Mrs. Davis and the cat in my room. If this <u>were</u> true, one of the Blacks would be dead by now, his snake-ass body hacked to pieces in my room. Since that night, I've seen two of 'em myself, and since the pieces of the rattler I chunked in the gunny sack didn't turn into a human carcass, like the one in Mr. Gunnison's story, I feel pretty confident that the other half-wit son is still roaming around the hills somewhere.

I'm sure that the Blacks are linked to

rattlesnakes, though, just like Mrs. Davis and the cats. I've got the incident at Jolley's Mercantile to go on, along with the rattler Pete and I saw on the road a few minutes before the Blacks tried to ambush us, and then the snake in my room at the end of that crazy Sunday. Ma said as much that night, after the two boarders had made it back to bed. I was afraid again that she was going to tell me to blow – hell, just in the past couple of weeks I'd shot up her place and filled it full of carbon tet, not to mention scared the stuffing out of everyone by impersonating a bloody corpse in the communal bathtub. No judge in the country would convict her if she wanted to give me the bum's rush.

So, around midnight, as I was stabbing pieces of snake with the end of my sheath knife and sacking them up while she swept and mopped up, I was half waiting for the axe to fall. She hadn't said much, but all of a sudden she shook her head and said, "That old man is pure-dee evil."

"Pardon me?" I said, looking up at her.

"Black. Pure evil. Nothin' but trash." She mopped vigorously at a bloody spot on the wood floor, a lock of hair coming undone and dangling in front of her forehead. "Always has been, always will be."

"You think it was Old Man Black who did this?"

She stopped mopping, fixing me with a stare. "What do <u>you</u> think, Robert?"

"I think it was him, Ma. Although I don't know how he managed to get up on the roof and let that snake in my room."

"Maybe not him. Maybe one of them kids done it. Don't matter. Dollars to doughnuts he was behind it. I guess you made him mad back there at the train station, th' night you come in." She fell silent for a short time, as we worked along, and then she added, "You be careful, Robert. He's gonna try again."

I nodded, skewering another piece of snake. "I will," I said. "I might even be able to give him a reason to leave me alone."

The opportunity to do that fell in my lap yesterday. I don't much believe in divine intervention, but you be the judge. It sure as hell seems like more than mere coincidence.

I was scheduled to go by Dr. Chavez's downtown office to get my stitches pulled out, so that morning I guided the big Indian into a parking space beside an old pick-up that looked familiar. Just as I got to the door of Doc's storefront, it opened and this big blond hulk lumbered out. He had no shirt on, his shoulder was bandaged, and right behind him was Old Man Black, a cigarette dangling from his lips.

Neither one recognized me at first. They were both a couple of steps past when Black turned and stared at me, jaw dropping, cigarette falling to the sidewalk.

His nitwit kid stopped too, eyes going over me like an animal's. His mouth twisted into an enraged scowl.

"You gawd damned—" He started to go for me then, but the old man put out a scrawny arm.

"I'm still alive," I told them, my screwed-up sense of the dramatic kicking in. I got to admit I postured a little, struck a pose. "Maybe you already knew that. I'm not even hurt much. But I <u>am</u> getting mad, and <u>some</u>body's going to be sorry."

I stood in the doorway for effect just a moment, and then shut it behind me before they could rush me. I didn't figure they'd start anything in the Doc's office, and I was right. Cracking the door after a few moments, I watched the two of them, jawing at one another, get in the ancient truck and drive away. When they were gone, I went back out and picked up Old Man Black's cigarette butt, twisting out the glowing end. Then, holding it by the ash end between thumb and forefinger, I walked back in.

I held it that way until the nurse came out for me. When she asked if I needed an ash tray, I told her no, and looking as though she thought I was a little nuts she led me into a well- organized room that seemed almost a carbon copy of the one in Doc Chavez's house. He was waiting for me.

"What you got there?" he asked, nodding at the cigarette butt I held.

"Something I'd like to put in a test tube. Can I get one from you?"

He looked at me for a long moment and then,

as if he'd just gotten my idea, suddenly grinned.

"You can go now, Ida." He nodded and the nurse slipped out the door. Then he turned back to me.

"Fresh?" he asked.

"You bet."

"Know what you're doing?"

"I think I do."

"All right then." He went to a cabinet and pulled out a test tube. There was a stopper in the top that he uncorked, holding the tube out to me. I dropped the butt in and he replaced the stopper.

"Here you go."

"Thanks, doc," I said, sticking the tube in the front pocket of my CCC shirt.

"Sit down over here and let me see if I can get those stitches out." Peeling off the bandage, he poked around a little. "Looks good. Looks good. Now this is going to hurt a little."

It did, but my mind wasn't on the pain. It was on what he said as he worked away.

"We know what you're doing, Mr. Brown, although we can't quite figure out how you know what you're doing – hold still, now. There." A snap, and I knew he'd popped one of the stitches. "Just don't get in too deep." Snap. "There's only so much help we can give you. We've existed like this for a lot of years, and too much boat-rocking doesn't help anybody. Still, I admire you. And I'm not the only one." Again, there was a little snapping sound, and before I knew it he was cleaning up the traces of the wound and putting on another, smaller bandage.

"That ought to do it," he said. "Give my receptionist two bucks on your way out and we'll call it square. Keep the dressing on for a couple more days and you'll be fine. It hardly left a scar."

I nodded. "Thanks for taking care of me, Dr. Chavez. I appreciate it." Then, "I suppose you've told me all you can tell me."

"I have," he returned. "And maybe a little more."

With those parting words, I nodded another thanks at him and left, remembering the test tube in my front pocket, knowing exactly what potentially boat-rocking thing I was going to do with its contents.

Your pal and faithful correspondent,

Robert

June 24. 1939, Saturday morning

Dear John,

I have really been ginning the folklore interviews out – fifteen in the last week alone.

Concentrating on them helps me forget all this stuff about the Blacks and the snakes and the cats for a while. When I'm typing up one of the reports, I can lose myself in it, just like you do in a good book or pulp.

The upshot is that I'm so ahead of schedule that I may actually get finished before the end of October. I think I wrote you that this WPA job is officially over on October 1 and my clerk's job in the Department of War begins very soon after that. Man, things are really speeding along. When I get settled in Washington, D.C., I want you to come stay with me a day or ten. Elaine could spare you for that long, and so could the paper, I bet. Maybe we'll take all this stuff I've been writing you about and make it into a book.

First of all, though, I've got to get through the rest of my time here with my carcass intact.

Things have been quiet since the confrontation between me and two-thirds of the Black clan at Doc Chavez's office Tuesday, when I had the presence of mind to go out and pick up the old man's cigarette butt. I've half expected something else to happen by now, although I haven't had any discernible seventh sense about it, which says something. And sure enough, it's been quiet. In a way, it's like they say in the western movies – too quiet. But in another way, it's been good. I've felt a sense of peace, although there's a little guilt mixed up in in, too, because of what I did with Old Man Black's cigarette butt. I don't want to tell you too much about that yet – not until I'm sure it's working.

I've had a lot of time to think about things while I've been out riding from place to place in the mountains, gathering up my interviews. There's no doubt that the "good" people in town – Ma, Mrs. Davis, the doc, even Pete – are trying to tell me what they can about the evil in Mackaville, which seems to center squarely around Old Man Black. And somehow, I know that the good people are in some way connected up with the cats that have bedeviled me since I pulled into this burg.

Yeah, the cats. Cuckoo as it sounds, I know the cats have something to tell me, too. Sometimes I think about you sitting there in your bungalow, or maybe in the Dispatch newsroom, reading one of my wilder letters and shaking your head. Maybe you laugh. I really do hope you think I'm not non compos mentis, or that I'm going to end up like Old Lady Crawford back in Hallock. Remember how we used to sneak up at night and throw rocks at the porch of her creepy old house, just so we could watch those dozens of cats shoot out from under it?

You know, I couldn't stop you from showing these letters to other people, but I hope you're not and I don't think you are. You are the one person I'd trust with my life, so I'm trusting you with all of this, too, and I'm trusting you to keep it to yourself for now. Just know it is happening exactly as I'm putting it down. I've been looking over your letters again and I can't see any sign that you think I've gone around the bend. I thank you for that.

Besides the people I mentioned, I think some other citizens of Mackaville and its mountainous environs are trying to tell me things in their own way. Did you notice that the snake-man in that story Mr. Gunnison told me was named "Black?" Sure, it's a common name, but rattlers and Blacks are so mixed up in this town that I think the old guy had a reason for using that name.

If a few of these old-timers I'm interviewing really are trying to communicate something to me, then I wonder what to make of the yarn I got yesterday. I put some brand-new carbon paper in the typer and punched out that damned second carbon copy for you, which I will send along in this letter so you can see it for yourself. Maybe you can give me some insight.

It came from an old woman named Mrs. Gabber. I'm pretty sure I wrote you earlier how I ran into one of the Gabbers about a month ago – the old boy who asked me if I was writing "hurtful" things – and how Pete explained to me about how

Gabber was a big name in Mackaville. She must be kind of a shirt-tail relation because she lives out in the hills under fairly modest circumstances – not dirt poor, but not rich either. She's got a clean little house and some pigs and chickens and a fair-sized truck patch, so I guess she does all right. She told me she's got lots of "relations" around. I know of at least two, because I accidentally made their acquaintance on the way up to her place.

I had taken a road that cut across the flank of one mountain, then hooked across a small saddle and wound on up and over another. The outlook was beautiful, and I was on some really lonely roads, the kind with grass growing up through the middle. Although I was keeping an eye out for snakes and Blacks, there didn't seem to be any, so maybe I got a little careless.

I'd bought a couple of bottles of Cleo Cola at Sparky's Market in town on the recommendation of old Sparky Winters himself, who told me "it's made right cheer in Arkansas, and it's better'n Coke." So I took a flyer on it. It's not "better'n Coke," but it's not half bad. "The Queen of Sparkling Drinks," according to the bottle, which also has a hotcha drawing of Cleopatra on it to make sure you get the idea.

I broke one out early, finished it in a few gulps, and swerved off onto the cliff side of the road and stopped, pitching the bottle out into space and listening to it crash on the rocks below. Then, out of my profound, natural modesty, I stepped across the road and into a bunch of pine trees before unbuttoning my fly to take a leak. Everything was kind of on a little flat or plateau here and the country dropped away gradually on the other side. The trees kept me from seeing that slope until I stepped into the woods. Then I realized I was peeing on a little path, not quite as wide as the road, running through the trees. Looking around, I saw a couple of sets of tracks, like train tracks, curling back and down through the pines, going out of sight behind a huge rock to the right of me that thrust up about twenty yards down the slope.

Well, <u>that</u> was interesting. Although I knew the Blacks or even snakes could be hiding behind it, and my .22 and shotgun were back in the sidecar, I was intrigued and stupid enough to step off down that little trail. Then I smelled something familiar – kind of like creamed-corn gone bad – and suddenly heard a "CLLLIIICK" behind me.

We've both read the books, seen the movies, heard the radio shows, but nothing, <u>nothing</u>, sounds as clear, as crisp, as deadly and purposeful and <u>personal</u> as a gun being cocked behind you. I raised my hands and then turned, very slowly I assure you, to face the music.

Even in those few seconds, though, I knew in my heart that it wasn't the Blacks. And the seventh sense was right again, along with another sense – my sense of smell. The odor, which had become familiar to me over the past few weeks, was that of sour mash. I'd stumbled onto a moonshine operation.

The man was middle-aged or a little older, dressed in overalls and a brown shirt, a soft cap pulled down over his forehead. At least a decade's-worth of handlebar mustache hung over his mouth and above the biggest damn Winchester rifle I'd ever seen.

"Whatcha doin' here, gummint man?" he asked, his mouth hanging open so much that I could see a huge chaw of masticated tobacco inside. It wasn't pretty. Neither was the tone of the question. In that moment, I questioned why I thought it was a good idea to still be wearing my CCC duds.

I swallowed.

John, there are times in life when God touches you. You and I have both been there, when we knew whatever we said would have a profound effect, good or bad, on our immediate situation and so the words had better be perfect. When that happens, sometimes you've got no choice but to throw a little prayer heavenward, open your mouth, and hope the exact right thing comes out. You and I have both wondered just how much God has to do with the minutiae in our lives, or anyone else's, but I've got little doubt that in a terrifying or life-threatening situation He might give a little aid.

I sure as hell figured this was one of those situations, especially when I blurted out, before I could even form a thought: "I'm lookin' to see if I kin buy some of thet 'shine." Just like that, in the vernacular and everything.

Were those words divinely inspired? I thought at the time that they were. I also thought that the grin that I suddenly felt on my face came from the same place. And I'd like to believe that together, the grin and the words saved me from a lonely unmarked grave deep in the Ozark Mountains. After all, I was still in the clothes I'd worked in from the beginning of my time in Mackaville; CCC outfit and boots and newsboy cap. For all they knew, I was a uniformed government agent come to bust up their still and haul 'em off to the pokey.

"Jube!" the guy hissed.

Jube? Now what the hell did that mean? I was racking my brain for obscure hill-billy terms when I heard a second voice behind me.

"It's that writer feller, I reckon," it said.

I resisted the impulse to whirl around, keeping my eyes on the man in front of me. His rifle hadn't moved.

"He's right," I said. "Mr. Jube is right. I'm on my way up to see Mrs. Ezekiel Gabber for a story." I'd inadvertently dropped the corn pone accent, but it was too late to pick it up now. "Then I got a whiff of your mash, and it smelled awful good." I actually licked my lips then – pure minstrel show but what the hell – before continuing.

"I figured to slip up on whoever was mixing

up this first-class hootch and see if maybe they wouldn't sell me a jar."

Were he and the guy behind me buying it? I wondered. If they weren't, it wasn't because I hadn't thrown everything I had into it.

The hill-billy stared at me for a moment, the rifle still aimed right at my clockworks.

"You couldn't slip up on nothin' ridin' that damned ol' motor bike. Sheeet, we heared you a mile away." He looked over my shoulder, speaking to the man I figured was Jube. "Granny say anything about this fella comin'?"

There was a step, and Jube materialized right beside me. His tanned, deeply wrinkled face was clean-shaven; that was about the only difference between him and a man I guessed was his brother. He wasn't carrying a rifle, though, which gave me some small comfort.

I jumped, doing my best Edgar Kennedy reaction. "Damn!" I said. "You sure move quiet." I was playing to my audience now, and I figured flattery couldn't hurt.

"Yeah, Jeb," he said, looking me up and down. "'Member? She's all fared up about it. Gonna tell 'im a damn good true story. 'Bout pigs and cats."

A freighted look seemed to pass between the two of them then, and Jeb lowered his Winchester.

"Yeah, I recollect that now," he said. "Guess he's all right then." He turned his gaze to me. "Ain't got none but our own personal supply right now, but we'll be pullin' a new batch in a couple of days. But we're business-men, you know. We'll give you a snort for free, so you'll know what yore gettin'. C'm'on."

He turned and started down the hill and I followed, wondering why he had suddenly lost his ignorant hill-billy accent. And I realized then that his flannel shirt had looked both new and expensive. I looked back at Jube, trailing behind us, and saw that his clothing fit that same pattern.

Then I suddenly got the distinct impression that these guys had just been screwing with me, putting on the exaggerated hill-billy talk and mannerisms to maybe throw a scare into this Yankee interloper. In fact, I realized these two could very well be the rich Gabbers who ran the town.

Within about fifty yards, we dropped into a deep ravine with a good-sized stream running through the bottom. The still was built into a rocky cleft above the water, the mash tanks up on the bank. The creamed-corn odor here was very nearly overpowering.

When we stopped, he turned toward me, holding out his hand, rifle cradled in his other arm. "Jeb Gabber," he said. "Gabber Meats."

So I was right.

"I'm Robert Brown," I said, "and I'm very glad to meet the men behind Mackaville's No. 1 employer."

I turned and shook hands with Jube, too, and they both broke out in laughter until tears came into their eyes. It kind of pissed me off, but I knew better than to say anything. In fact, I played right along and grinned at them like the Cheshire Cat.

"Didn't fool you, huh?" asked clean-shaven Jube between bursts of laughter.

"Sure you did," I said. "I don't mind saying you scared the hell out of me. If you'd tightened the screws just a little bit more, I might've run all the way back to Minnesota."

My statement brought on another round of mirth, and Jeb was still laughing as he reached down into the stream and produced a jug.

"This here is the special stuff – triple-distilled," he said, uncorking the jug and passing it to me.

I nodded. "Thanks," I said, and tipped the jug up.

The mountain dew at Jolley's Mercantile had tasted like gasoline. This stuff made it seem as meek as sarsaparilIa. I had no choice but to suck it down, taking Lord knows how much of the lining of my mouth and throat along with it. Tears erupted in my eyes. If someone had waved a match front of my face, my breath would've exploded.

"Gentlemen, have *mercy*!" I gasped, adding only a little theatricality. "I'm just a tender child. You must've squeezed that panther piss out of a *rattlesnake*!" I hoped they didn't mind the mixed metaphor.

They didn't. I guess they'd expected a reaction from this uniformed city boy, because they'd been watching me pretty intently when I took hold of that jug. After my histrionic response, they both exploded with hilarity again, and I joined in the laughter myself, tears still rolling down my cheeks from the gulp of 'shine. Then they each helped themselves to a snort, and by the time Jube recorked the jug and set it back in the stream they had told me how to get to their farm – just down the road from Mrs. Gabber's, where I happened to be headed – and to show up there Sunday or Monday if I wanted a Mason jar full of fresh triple-distilled shine.

"It's the least we can do," Jube said, with barely a hint of Arkansas drawl, "seeing as how we had a little fun with you and all."

I thanked them both and climbed up on the big Indian. As I roared away, my feelings were curiously mixed. It had all been a joke, sure, but I wanted to like those two more than I did, if that makes any sense. In this town, it'd be best to stay on the good side of the Gabber family. But still, there was something about them that I just didn't like. Maybe *trust* describes the feeling better.

I headed on up to my interview feeling weirdly light-headed. Just one gulp of that witch's brew had been enough to kind of disconnect me from reality, and then Mrs. Gabber insisted I try some of her wild grape wine, which was damn good. Luckily, I didn't partake until I'd taken down her story; even then, thanks to the 'shine and the wine, that weird shorthand we invented came out even weirder, and I found it damn near impossible to decipher it when I got back last night. So I arose early this morning, a little bit worse for wear, and typed it up. There were a few words I wasn't sure about, but I think I got it ok. You be the judge.

By the way – that old Gabber I encountered last month at Pete's Skelly station. He's one of her first cousins, she told me. Jube and Jeb are sure enough her grandkids. Hell, everyone in this whole damn neck of the woods is likely related in some way or another.

Funny, though. You'd think with rich grandkids that the old lady would live more palatially than most of the other folks I've interviewed. But her home, while clean and comfortable, isn't very big or splashy. Maybe it's got a little more space, but otherwise there's nothing about it to make it stand out.

I'm headed into town now, so I'll get this mailed – even though I can't shake a growing mistrust of Postmaster Gibson – and then take a gander at the rack of used pulps at Sparky's Market. Since I've got a little bit of dough threatening to erupt into flame in my pocket, I might go by the town's other restaurant and get a hamburger. I've been in a couple of times and I really like the proprietor, an older Greek man named Castapolous who's had some adventures in his life.

All this government geetus makes me think like a Rockefeller. Hell, I might even drop by the drug store and see if there's a pulp I want badly enough to pay full price. I know if I was to buy one – or even two – I'd still have enough left over to take Patricia to the local movie palace tonight (admission is 50 cents at the Palace, as opposed to 25 at the Maribel) and buy her a box of Jujubes or whatever she wanted. (When we're at the Palace, she gets Sno-Caps, which they don't have at the Maribel.) And she is a whole other story that'll have to wait for another day.

Let's just say that when you visit me in Washington there's a chance someone else could be there, too.

It's funny. Right after I typed the part about going into town, I had a little bit of seventh sense blow through me like a zephyr. Probably it was warning me about something.

I guess I'll find out. And if whatever it is doesn't kill me, you will, too.

Let me know what you think of the enclosed tale, supposedly true.

Your pal and faithful correspondent,

Robert

WORKS PROGRESS ADMINISTRATION--FEDERAL WRITERS' PROJECT
Official Form

DATE: 23 June 1939
INTERVIEWER: R.A. Brown
STORY TOLD BY: Mrs. Ezekiel (Alta) Gabber
AGE: 90
ADDRESS: Star Route 2, Mackaville, Arkansas

Hit was 1846 when Jon Bodeen up and as't Silvee Lower to marry 'im. Jon Bodeen was my gran'-pappy. They wuz a handsome couple. He was a big man, nigh onto six feet, and she was a cotton headed li'l woman with snappin' blue eyes. In due time, a big bouncin' boy wuz borned to 'em and they wuz as happy as two humins ever wuz. They made over they chile like everything and 'loved he was the most beautiful boy ever borned.

He had a li'l crib of a bed right night to thar bed and eny sound a'tall would fetch one uv 'em up to his little side. He was a-doin' jest fine 'til one night in a rain storm a big crack o'lightnin' woke up Silvee and she woke up Jon 'cause she'd all of a sudden heered this big cat yowl right nearby. They looked and they was a big ole white cat a-sittin' on thet baby's chest jest a-suckin' out its breath.

Jon swooped his arm acrosst the crib an' threw thet cat a-squallin'. Afore he could get to his feet, it had clumb up th' door and squeezed through th' keyhole. Yep. A big ol' cat like thet. Ain't no tellin' how it happened, some kinda witchery he figgered, but my gran'pappy swore 'til he wuz in th' ground that he seen it jest that way.

Then he seen granny cuddlin' th' little baby an' screamin' like a banshee. Thet baby wuz stone cold dead and them two just about pined away with it.

Howsumever, Silvee had annuther baby boy th' next year. But they was powerful skairt that ole witch-cat, which is what they figgered it was 'cause of goin' through th' keyhole an' all, would come back an' try ta get they second child.

Now Jon's daddy lived pret' near 'em, and he knowed all about what had happened to that there first-born of Jon and Silvee's. Onced they second babe was borned, he tole 'em he was gonna move in with 'em and take care of thet ole witch-cat himself. Silvee weren't none too sure 'bout that, they cabin bein' so small and all, but Jon's daddy jest laughed and said he prob'ly weren't gonna be there long an' jest fer the nights.

So he started comin' down ev'ry night, jest as th' sun were goin' down, and stayin' right by thet baby's crib. I 'spect he'd been a-stayin' there 'bout three-four months when another big gully-washer come up durin' a pitchy-black night and Silvee and Jon woke up to the yowl of a cat.

'Course, they was skeered to death it was happenin' agin, so they jumped up like they was one and saw that same ole cat a-sittin' on they dear baby's chest, just like before.

Then, like he'd come in on the wind, outta nowhere, the front door flew open an' a big ole razorback hog jumped up into thet little crib and snapped his jaws around thet ole cat's head.

Thet ole cat screamed as the jaws crunched down, and then that beast shook his head and threw th' cat plumb outta th' crib onto th' dirt floor. Afore either Jon or Silvee could say anything atall, thet big hog had whipped outta there, took up thet dead cat in its mouth, and scampered out th' door inta the storm.

By this time, thet baby was a-wailin' fierce and Jon and Grandmammy Silvee was a- fussin' and cryin' and carryin' out, so glad they boy weren't dead. It took 'em a while afore they realized Jon's daddy weren't there neither.

They sat there for a long time, makin' over th' baby, and then suddenly they was a thund'rous knock at the door. Jon grabbed up his rifle afore openin' up, and when he did there standed his daddy, my great-grandpappy, and he told 'em that ole witch-cat was roastin' in Hell and wouldn't be botherin' 'em no more.

He said he'd go back to his own cabin as soon as th' rain let up.

Silvee, holdin' her child tight, thanked her daddy-in-law oh so pretty. Then she taked a corner of her night shirt and cleaned the blood offen the side of his mouth.

June 25, 1939, Sunday morning

Dear John,

Thanks for your latest missive. Although you didn't say anything to make me think this way, I realized as I was reading it that I haven't always thanked you for being a pal and supporting me and not thinking I'm crazy as a tree full of hoot owls – or, if you do, not telling me about it. I've been so full up with what's going on with <u>me</u> that I've hardly acknowledged the news and observations you've sent in your own letters.

I apologize and I'll try to do better, even though I know it probably doesn't matter much to you. I do appreciate that you're keeping everything I write. You have the only copies of the letters. I could make carbons, but after all that lunacy with the cat in my room looking at my interview notes I decided not to keep anything around that might tempt the forces-that-be in this town. Now that I think about it, I guess some sharp customer could glean something from looking at your letters to me, which I'm keeping in my top bureau drawer, but I don't think it'd be much. I looked them over again several days ago and you don't get real specific about my experiences here, which is good.

Anyhow, you might think about being even <u>less</u> specific from here on out, just as a precaution. Make it so we'll both know what you're talking about, but if someone should snatch 'em, <u>he</u> wouldn't.

Sorry to be a pain, but it just seems prudent to do it this way.

And now, I'll let you know that my seventh sense was right again.

When I finished up writing you yesterday morning, it was already warm but not very humid, and a nice breeze was blowing out of the east that wafted any packing-house smell out into the mountains. Things are still green around here, pretty, and on the walk I had that good God-is-in-his-heaven feeling that made me feel like a kid again.

I mailed your letter at the p.o. and then headed across the street to Foreman's Drug Store to check the pulp rack and enjoy a cherry phosphate. I was doing just that when someone slammed me hard from behind, almost knocking me into the magazine stand. I'd already slurped down most of the phosphate, but the force of the open-handed blow threw ice from the glass in all directions.

I looked up into this big dull face, piggy blue eyes squinting under a shock of matted blond hair. And I knew my days of being free from the Blacks had come to an end.

"Whatcha doin' ta Pa, ya dumb shit?" he muttered, fire in his eyes. His breath could've run off a buzzard.

Fishing an ice cube out of my uniform pocket, I did some fast thinking, coming to the conclusion that, sometimes, you just have to step into the arena.

"I'll tell you exactly what I'm doing," I returned, locking eyes with him. "Step outside and I'll explain – and then I'll take you on in a clean fight."

He didn't expect that. Bullies never do. He goggled at me.

"We'll settle this – like men," I added.

I turned toward the door, placing my glass and stray ice cubes on the chromium top of the soda fountain and hoping he wouldn't grab me from behind. It had gotten real still in the drug store. With each step I took, the spilled ice under my shoes seemed to explode like fire-crackers.

I heard him snort behind me but pushed on without looking back. The little bell on the screen door clinked as I exited, but the door didn't shut. He was right behind me.

As soon as I stepped through that doorway, I took a fast leap to the side and jumped out onto the sidewalk. It was a good move, too, because he had both ham hands reaching for me and he almost lost his balance as he grabbed thin air. I laughed when he stumbled and his face went blood crimson. He almost roared as he came for me.

Lots of things flew through my head then. I thought of that first fight I'd had with this gee and his brother, a hundred years ago on the train platform. I tried to remember what punches I'd used. And then, crazily, I remembered a name: Seth. Was that his name, or the name of the brother Pete had winged up in the mountains? I'd been thinking of 'em as Tweedledum and Tweedledee for so long I had no idea.

Then he swung, and my thoughts turned to pure-dee survival.

He was fast, but awkward, grabbing at me with his left hand while throwing the hook at me with his right. I ducked and bobbed away from his swing, stepped to the side, and uncorked a hard left to his nose. It was the same punch I'd landed back there at the depot, and it had pretty much the same effect. The sodden crunch under my fist felt grand. Before I backed away, I threw a right at his Adam's apple, hitting it dead on. The punch had some zip to it, and he staggered back, gagging and gasping.

I couldn't help it if the stupid bastard didn't know how to box. He had me overmatched in height and reach and weight, and I had to do what I could. I weaved toward him and he started windmilling like a kid on a playground, graceless as a charging elephant. I got in too close, and a lucky punch from one of those leg-sized arms caught me under the chin, knocking me off balance. I staggered just long enough for him to pop me hard under the ribs. I sucked hard for air, caught another blow on the shoulder that sent waves of pain through me. Then I got in a solid right to his hard belly and sent another left over his guard to close one of his piggy eyes.

He stumbled back into a parked jalopy then, leaning up against it, tried to catch his breath. I was aware of people all around us, frozen like figures in a painting, all eyes on me and my combatant. I glimpsed, or thought I did, some sort of uniformed guy with a gun and holster, but he didn't make any move toward us. For a moment, I'd thought he was Sheriff Meagan, who I half-hoped would make a deus ex machina appearance like he'd done my first night in town. But we'd gotten so far now I knew that whatever he could do might not be enough to stop this melee.

These thoughts raced through my head as I dove in on my opponent, not giving him a second to recover, shooting straight, hard-line punches from the shoulder that sometimes hit his arms but just as often slammed through to his sternum or face. He was sagging and I knew I had him when I saw, out of the corner of my eye, one of those painted background figures moving toward me. I jerked my head around just as his idiot brother swung hard at me with his good hand, his right, the other one still poking out of Doc Chavez's sling. It swished past my nose like a Lefty Grove fastball.

Right about that time, I stopped half-hoping and started half-praying for Sheriff Meagan and his Remington .44 to make an appearance. It was now two on one, and I knew having one arm out of commission didn't mean a hell of a lot to this yahoo. I was in for it unless I could somehow get the best of the situation, and I mean in a hurry.

That thought came to an abrupt end when my first assailant – let's call him Seth, whether he was or not – found the juice to raise up and land a good one on my right cheek while I was momentarily distracted by his brother. I danced back, my ears ringing, eyes watering.

I had to stay out of the other Black's grasp. Even with one arm, he could reach around and pin me to his body, and as soon as Seth got his feet back under him, I'd be hamburger meat.

So I made a tactical decision to back off quickly into the street. Seth had pulled himself up from the side of the parked auto and was teetering on his feet as his brother stalked toward me, his good hand balled into a hard fist.

I forced myself to smile, holding my palms upward as he approached. I backed around a little, until I was between him and Seth. A plan had suddenly formed in my mind.

"Listen," I said, gasping a little. "This is silly. There's no need to fight. Hell, it's not fair. You've only got one good arm."

I dropped my hands as he stopped right in front of me, hand cocked, momentarily unsure. His astonishment didn't last long. But it was long enough. I grabbed the front of his shirt with both hands and threw myself backward, pulling him down with me. As we fell, I stuck my right foot into his belly for leverage and just as we hit the pavement I pushed up and off. It was beautiful. He sailed over me, screaming like a woman, and, as I had hoped, cannonballed right into his staggering brother. They both slammed against the car in a heap, and I jumped up and started throwing punches as hard as I could into the brother I'd just launched with my little jiu- jitsu technique. I didn't let up until he'd slumped to the pavement, lying atop his twin.

I have no doubt they would've been ready for another round in a few minutes, but I didn't wait to find out if I was right. I pulled myself together, stiffened my back, and walked right across that street without so much as a rearward glance. Once I'd gone a couple of blocks and felt I was far enough away, I ducked into an alley and let myself sag against the brick wall of the Mackaville bank for a minute or two. I hurt in a dozen places and knew I'd have a first-class shiner in the morning. When I started off again I was limping, too. Suddenly, I was very, very tired and something else – homesick, maybe, as funny as that sounds. I started thinking about all those people who watched as those two big oafs took me on and didn't do one damn thing about it. I felt alone and I wanted to go home. To Minnesota, I mean. To my people and my friends.

Instead, I limped on down to Pete's, and pretty soon I felt better. While I told him the story of the fight, he cleaned up a cut on my cheek I didn't even know I had and gave me four aspirin that I washed down with a Coke from his pop box. I had a couple more Cokes and by that time I felt better, good enough to watch the pumps while Pete went down to Castapolous's place, which he likes better than the Busy Bee too, and got a sack of hamburgers. I'd planned to work for him for a couple of hours that day before going back to Ma's to clean up for my Saturday night date with Patricia. I didn't want to have to break another one because of those damn Blacks.

The folks started coming by before Pete got back. I guess word had gotten out that I was at the station. Some of 'em bought gas, sure enough, but more just wanted to shake my hand and congratulate me on the fight. When Pete got back from the cafe and saw what was going on, he started kidding me about a rematch so that he could have a tire sale.

Of course, I kept an eye out for the Black twins, but apparently they'd had enough because they never showed. I'd be lying if I said I wasn't relieved as hell when it came time to leave and they still hadn't shown up. I don't run away from fights, John, as you know, but I wasn't quite in shape for another bout right then.

Sheriff Meagan did show up, a couple of hours after I'd hoped to see him and his revolver back there in the middle of town. I was standing beside the pumps with Pete when the sheriff climbed out of his black sedan and walked over to us, shaking his head slowly.

"Guess you decided not to take my advice, huh?" he said to me.

"You mean about walking softer?" I asked, remembering our conversation a few nights earlier outside the doc's house. "Sheriff, I was walking soft as a kitten. I wasn't looking for anything but a new pulpwood magazine to read. You can ask anyone who was in Foreman's when that big palooka started in on me."

"Done asked 'em," he said, looking me up and down. "You hurt?"

"Not mortally."

A flicker of a grin played across his broad face, and he looked at Pete. "You've got a hell of a specimen here," he said, nodding at me.

"He's a dandy," returned Pete noncommittally, pulling out his rag and wiping at an oily spot on the top of a pump.

A car pulled up on the other side, and the old fellow in the driver's seat grinned and gave me a wave. "Nice goin' downtown," he half-hollered out the car window as Pete went over to wait on him. I nodded my thanks and turned back to Sheriff Meagan, just in time to hear him tell me, "You're a regular damn hero, Brown."

I couldn't tell if it was praise or scorn.

"Wasn't trying to be," I said. "I was just trying not to get killed. How're my adversaries?"

"Dunno. They was gone by the time I got back in town. Been out in the country since dawn lookin' for hog rustlers. I could go ahead and visit the Black place, but I figure if either one of 'em was dead or dyin' I'd hear about it."

"You got a deputy?" I asked him suddenly.

His eyes narrowed. "Nope. Why?"

"I thought maybe I saw a lawman in the crowd downtown. He didn't make any move to break things up, though."

"The Mackaville po-lice," he said, deliberately exaggerating that first syllable with a long "o." Whatever else he was, Sheriff Meagan was no hayseed. "Wasn't the chief – he'd have waded right in. But a couple of the others, hell, they might grab a bag of peanuts and settle in to watch."

Still, I was surprised. "Aren't they supposed to keep the peace in town, like you do in the county?"

"Oh, yeah," he said, emphasizing the word just enough for me to understand he didn't think much of the Mackaville constabulary. I started to say something else, but he beat me to it.

"Guess you know ol' man Black's sick as a dog."

"I didn't, no."

"Yeah. Doc says he can't find anything wrong, but th' ol' degenerate's hurtin' all right. Sharp pain in his chest that don't go 'way. Them big mulletheaded boys told Doc his medicine wasn't doin' no good and they was going to find somethin' at the drug store to give 'im. Guess that's how they ran into you."

"I wasn't looking for trouble, like I said. I was just looking at the new magazines and drinking a cherry phosphate."

"I know. You didn't start it, neither. But now you're the big hero." He took his big cowboy hat off and wiped his brow.

"Jus' remember," he said, refitting the hat, "a lot of these citizens who're comin' by an' makin' a big to-do over you about all this are the same ones who woulda stood there while them Blacks pounded you into cornmeal mush, if that's the way it had went. Maybe the *po*-lice would've finally gotten 'round to steppin' in, but I wouldn't count on it. You ain't one of th' locals, and when it comes right down to th' nut-cuttin', there ain't very many gonna jump in to help you against the Blacks nor no one else from these parts. Folks ain't warm toward the Blacks, but you ain't number one on their hit parade, neither, 'cause they still ain't so damn sure 'bout you. Keep that in mind, huh?"

"I will," I told him. "But you, and Pete here—" I nodded toward Pete, who was hanging up the gas nozzle "—and Ma Stean. I can count on *you*, right?"

I saw a look pass between Pete and the Sheriff before the latter said, dyspeptically, "Sure. Long's you keep on the straight an' narrow, anyway. But I ain't sayin' we're always gonna be around to pull your fat outta the fire."

"I know," I said, thinking about how I'd

hoped to see him when the trouble started with the Blacks.

"Just try to stay outta trouble, son," he added as he began ambling back across the drive, over to his jet-black Buick. When he opened it up to get in, there was an explosion of sunlight, reflected by the big painted-on gold star splashed across the outside of his front door.

"I've *been* trying," I shouted at him, shielding my eyes from the sudden flash. "Honest."

He shook his head a third time, with what looked like a ghost of a smile playing briefly across his broad face. Then he shut the door and drove away.

I knew what he meant about the people who would've stood by and let the Black twins take me apart. I was sure some of the well-wishers had earlier been a part of that oil-painting background surrounding me during the fight. He was right. They were no particular friends of the Blacks, but at best they weren't sure what to make of the tall outsider in the CCC uniform.

Still, I got the feeling their congratulations were genuine. So maybe they were just intimidated by the Blacks, like downtown Mackaville was a schoolyard full of cowed kids and the oafish twins were the top bullies on the playground. I shared that thought with Pete, and he allowed as to how there might be something to it. He'd just begun to elaborate when two more cars came rolling in and we got busy. Before I knew it, it was time for me to go, and I said goodbye while he was still servicing a '32 Dodge driven by an old dark guy in bib overalls and straw hat – who waved at me as I left and hollered, "Good fightin', young'un!"

I got cleaned up and took the Indian over to the Davis house, where Patricia was waiting for me. She and Mrs. Davis must've been about the only two people in Mackaville who hadn't heard about the fight, and while I tried to soft-pedal it she made over the wound on my cheek and my blackening eye.

At least the dust-up with the Blacks had given me some status around town. The teenaged boys who tried to be vaguely menacing every time I showed up with Patricia at one of the town's movie houses were, instead, almost comically deferential toward me, nodding their hellos and practically bowing when they stepped aside to let us pass. I strutted through them, wearing my shiner like a badge of honor.

A film called Sergeant Madden, with Wallace Beery as a hard-boiled cop, was playing at the Palace, and I would've been happy with that, but to my surprise Patricia told me she liked horse operas so we went to the Maribel instead and took in a Poverty Row double-feature: Texas Wildcats, a sagebrusher with Tim McCoy as a government agent who becomes a masked vigilante; and Heroes of the Marne, a French film about a big rich farmer whose life is changed when the Great War breaks out. Even though they put in American voices on the soundtrack, the second one was pretty slow going, especially after a McCoy western, and I found my mind wandering. I thought about how much prettier Patricia was than any of the women up there on the screen. Then I started thinking about what Sheriff Meagan had told me earlier that day.

Surely, I thought, Patricia and her grandmother would be two I could count on, wouldn't they? I glanced over at her, and she caught my eye and smiled back at me, her head nestled in the crook of my arm.

Then my mind rambled back to the fight, and to what the Black goon had said to me there in Foreman's, after trying to shove my shoulder blades through my chest with one pop.

Whatcha doin' ta Pa?

And the sheriff, telling me that Old Man Black was sick.

The evidence was still circumstantial, but I was just about ready to accept it, if only because it would mean that what I'd done with the cigarette butt – and part of a nine-cent block of paraffin wax from Sparky's Market – was working.

Your cryptic pal,

Robert

June 25, 1939, Sunday night

Dear John,

How about this? Two letters from me in the same day. I wonder if they'll both get to St. Paul at the same time. Let me know if they do or don't.

I wanted to tell you about a couple of things that happened today, one more or less normal and one that's pretty wild, which means "normal" for Mackaville, I guess. I'll take them in order.

First, I finally gave in to Ma Stean's urgings and went to church. Well, the real reason I went is that Patricia brought it up last night after our date, and at this point I'd probably do anything she asked me to do. Don't tell Ma Stean, but the beautiful sweet Patricia is why my bony ass was fitted into a pew at the Mackaville Presbyterian Church this morning. It's one of the three big churches in Mackaville, the others being the Methodist and the Baptist. I wrote you real early on about the Baptist church; it's the one near downtown, the first one I saw after I hit Mackaville. Since then, I've found out there's a little bitty Catholic congregation, too, and some splinter churches in converted houses or under brush arbors outside of town around the foothills. Probably more out in the mountains.

The Presbyterians have a nice old building of gray granite blocks, what I'd call colonial style, with great columns in the front and a tall tower steeple. The main part is a big hall – a sanctuary is the proper term, I think – with a couple of wings in the back for Sunday school classes. In front was a place for people to park their cars and tie their horses, and both jalopies and horse-drawn wagons – along with a couple of saddled ponies – occupied most of it by the time I pulled up, chauffeuring everyone in Ma's car. Patricia pointed out a nice house next door where the preacher and his family lived, telling me the church provided it.

The message and order of worship were all kind of like we used to get back home at the Lutheran church in Hallock. Maybe I expected some pulpit-pounding and hellfire and brimstone, and I guess I would've gotten that from the Baptists or holy rollers, but this guy never even raised his voice. His message was about how we're going to be surprised at who we see in Heaven, so we'd better do like Jesus said and treat everybody like we would ourselves.

You've heard that line about preaching to the choir. Well, this congregation seemed to be practicing what he preached, especially when it comes to treating black folks as equals. I looked around a couple of times during his sermon and noticed several what looked to be full-blooded Negroes sitting with everybody else, not in back or anything, but scattered throughout the pews. Here I am in the South, a region very tough on colored people, and I'm witnessing a mingling of the races we don't even see up in Minnesota. I remember hearing or reading something about how the Presbyterians split into Northern and Southern branches on account of slavery and the Civil War, and this has to be one of the Southern churches, but they treat coloreds just like anyone else. Of course, this is Mackaville, and I've found out that different rules apply in this burg than they do in the rest of the whole damn country. I guess since most of the population is at least some black, having full-black people as their equals makes sense. And now that I think about it, I've seen blacks and whites together in town, and Pete always treats them just like he would anybody else. Of course, he's got those full-blood colored relatives and so does just about everybody else here. Even Patricia.

So it might not make sense anywhere else on God's green earth, but it does in Mackaville, and by damn, if you hold it up and look at it, I think it makes pretty good sense to treat everybody the same, like you'd want to be treated. The Golden Rule, that's all this is.

Or maybe I've just "gone native."

The preacher, a middle-aged guy with a full head of curly hair who had that same coffee-and-cream skin color as most of the townspeople, went from talking about heaven to talking about FDR, and how we had to be our brothers' keepers and that meant keeping the Democrats in office. I'm not kidding. This guy talked about the good works Roosevelt was doing, God protect him (I can't help but agree), and how we all needed to support his efforts. I was pretty surprised by this blatant politicking, but the congregation seemed to take it in stride.

I guess I was the only one in that crowd of maybe a hundred who hadn't been there before, and when the preacher asked if there were any announcements Ma Stean stood up and introduced me as a visitor.

"This here's Robert Brown," she said, her voice slightly raised. "Some of you might already know 'im." Everybody started clapping then, and she whispered to me to stand up. I did, nodding my acknowledgement and feeling a little self-conscious about my black eye, which was already rimmed with yellow. I don't know if they were clapping because they knew about the fight yesterday or just due to the fact that they didn't get many visitors. Either way, it was a neat moment, shiner and all.

During the last hymn, "God be With You 'til We Meet Again," the minister walked up through the congregation and stood at the door to say goodbye to everyone. There was an informal aspect to that and I liked it. I followed Ma, Mrs. Davis, and Patricia out. I was wearing civilian clothes, khaki slacks with a shirt and tie – except for the tie, just what I wear when I take Patricia to the movies – but even dressed up I felt, I don't know, a little unworthy of the luminous young lady in front of me. She is just beautiful, and smart beyond her years. I really want you to meet her.

Anyhow, when it came my time, the preacher grabbed my hand with enthusiasm and pumped away. "Son, I sure wish I'd had a bet on that fight!" he said. "You really surprised those ol' twins." He was loud enough that several people milling around on the steps looked at me, and I could see that if they hadn't yet made the connection between this duded-up guy and the fellow in the CCC uniform who'd fought the Blacks – even with the cut on the cheek and my blackened eye to give it away – they understood it now. Before I could get down the steps, I was surrounded by well-wishers, some of whom I recognized from the day before. One of them was an old guy dressed all in white, with white moustaches and a little Van Dyke beard. I'd seen him in the drug store, waiting on customers, and sure enough he turned out to be Mr. Foreman, the owner. He thanked me for taking the fight outside and added something about how I gave "those stinkin' Blacks" a lesson they needed.

Truth to tell, his words and all the attention kind of embarrassed me. "I got real lucky," I said, and then, "Anyone know if they're all right?"

At that, the talking around me just kind of paused. After a couple of moments, the preacher stepped over and took me to one side. "No bones broken, I understand," he said softly. "Seth, the one who started it, is gonna be sore as hel

— I mean, the devil — for a week or two. Sam, the one with the bad arm, is bruised up a little, but he just mostly had the wind knocked out of 'im. That's how I hear it, anyway."

"Okay. Thanks."

"You really care?" he asked in the same gentle tones.

"Yeah," I said. "I do. It's like you said in your sermon. I try to treat people the way I want to be treated, and I'm not really a fighter. I mean, I've learned how to fight in the past few years, because I would've gotten the bejabbers knocked out of me if I hadn't. But I grew up real skinny and I'm used to settling things with words. I still think that's the better way."

He clasped me on the shoulder and grinned. "That's a good attitude to have, son," he said. He probably wasn't any older than Sheriff Meagan, who called me "son" sometimes, too. But I didn't mind. "Glad to have you with us," he added, and that made me feel pretty good.

He went back to working his flock and I was looking for Patricia in the crowd when someone tapped me on the shoulder. It was Mr. Foreman. "Do you have a minute?" he asked, almost whispering.

"Sure," I returned, wondering what he wanted.

I soon found out. Mr. Foreman took me out to a nearly new Chevy Coupe pick-up and led me around to the driver's side, where we were more or less out of sight of the rest of the folks.

Climbing in, he reached under the seat and held out a paper sack.

"Here," he said, "Rights of combat, and well-earned."

It was good bourbon, smooth-drinking, especially after that alcohol-flavored kerosene that Dill Jolley and the Gabbers had shared with me. I took a good pull, and when I handed it back to Mr. Foreman I realized that a crowd of men had gathered around. I even saw an ebony face or two.

There was an old man standing next to me, and I passed the camouflaged bottle to him. He took a solemn drink and passed it to the next man.

It was the ritual we've seen back home, growing up, watching our dads and their pals coming in from hunting or fishing or some other big group activity, but this marked my first time as a participant. And not only that. Mr. Foreman and the rest were honoring me by giving me the bottle first. I expect you'll laugh, but I was real proud.

The bottle passed around and went back to Mr. Foreman, who held it out to me again. "Thanks," I said, grinning, "but I've got some women to escort home. I'd better be able to drive in a straight line." I reached in my pocket and pulled out a little envelope. "Lucky I've got some Sen-Sen," I added, shaking out a couple of squares.

They laughed, and I felt pretty damn happy with the world as I offered the Sen-Sen around.

As far as these fellows were concerned, I was a good man, no matter where I was from, good enough to be one of them. It was a hell of a feeling that stayed with me all the way to Mrs. Davis's house, where Ma and I had been invited for a pork-roast dinner.

It was delicious and I could've hung around there until dark, just to be near Patricia, but I didn't want to overstay my welcome. Also, I had a full schedule of interviews I wanted to get done in the next week, and I knew if I didn't get up to the Gabber place for my jar of 'shine today, I'd likely not be able to make it for several days. These hill folks take commitments seriously, and I'd made one to the Gabber boys.

So, reluctantly, I excused myself about an hour after dinner. Patricia followed me out to the big Indian.

"What's so important that you have to leave me?" she asked coyly, smiling a youthful smile that could've melted Adolf Hitler's heart.

I couldn't help it. I leaned over and kissed her on the lips, right there in daylight.

"Robert!" she said, pulling away – but not immediately – and glancing back at the house. "You want Gramma to see us?"

"I'll bet Gramma knows. She's pretty foxy."

"Still." She put a hand on my shoulder, squeezing it. "You need to be more careful. You're not very careful at all."

"I'll try to do better. For you," I said. "Look here."

From the sidecar, I pulled out a leather aviator's helmet, with goggles, which I'd mail-ordered from a military surplus catalog. "Just got it in." I put it on, adjusting the chin strap. I turned to her.

"What do you think?" I asked.

She smiled again. "Very handsome. Like Charles Lindbergh."

"Thank you."

As I climbed on the bike she looked back at the house, and then damned if she didn't lean over quick as a wink and kiss me again. I just about floated all the way to the Gabbers' place – and it wasn't a short trip. They lived up on Witch Mountain, although the name isn't as portentous as you might think. So far, I've heard about or driven on at least four other Witch Mountains within ten miles or so of Mackaville.

I wanted to think a lot about Patricia on the trip, so I was trying to keep all else out of my head, including the sense seeping into me that something wasn't right – that I might be heading for something bad again. As the old Indian growled up the road, I was sure I saw something moving in the brush at least a couple of times, down low. I felt eyes on me. Was it the seventh sense? Not to give anything away, but taking into consideration what happened later on, I think there's a good chance.

This Witch Mountain made for a beautiful drive, with steep drop-offs, rocky cliffs, and plenty of sharp curves to keep me on my toes.

The road that wound up to the Gabber boys' place seemed lonely and more tree-shaded than usual, but when I got there I saw they had a good-sized farm, spread across the head of a beautiful green valley. The second thing I saw was that there were all kinds of pigs running wild behind their whitewashed picket fence. I say "wild." What I mean is, they were like big friendly dogs – most of them.

I didn't know that at first. The farm and its two nearly identical houses – considerably bigger than their grandmother's place but not particularly ostentatious – sat a few hundred feet apart, back from the fence down a long pathway. When I opened up the gate to let myself in, all of a sudden I was surrounded by these porkers. There must've been fifty of them, and while they didn't attack me or anything like that, they showed no fear at all.

I can't say the same for me. I had never seen pigs so unafraid of a human, and their boldness gave me the creeps. A couple of big black boars even nudged my leg as I climbed back on the Indian. Remembering the pigs at the Murray farm back home, I pulled off my helmet and waved it at the two. They backed up then, and I drove on up on the gravel drive to the house on the left. When I got off the bike, those two big boar hogs were right there behind me, hanging back, watching my every move with bright little eyes.

Jube, the clean-shaven one, was standing on the porch, a white-haired woman in a faded-blue flour-sack dress holding onto his arm. He was grinning. I stopped the bike and looked around at the pigs.

"They figured you brought 'em something," he said loudly, above the noise of the pigs. "Either that, or they wanna see how the WPA tastes." He laughed then, just like he'd done when I'd taken that gulp of 'shine down by their still.

I had to laugh, too. Hell, John, those pigs surrounded me, acting just like farm dogs. I swatted one gently on the butt with my leather helmet and they all squealed. The one I'd hit drew up next to me like he was grateful for the attention. The only ones that weren't friendly were those two bristle-back boars, practically as big as my motorcycle, who stood off to the side watching with what seemed to me like an ugly attitude. I wondered what they'd do if I made a serious-looking grab at one of the smaller pigs, but I didn't want to know badly enough to actually do it.

When I stepped up onto the porch, the pigs drifted away, still hanging around near the house. I shook hands with Jube and introduced myself to his wife, who kind of uncertainly took my hand as well. We talked a little bit about the pigs – many of them, I found out, with upcoming dates at the Mackaville packing plant – and then Jeb wandered over from the house next door with a jar full of white lightning.

"You sure that stuff won't eat through the

glass before I can get it home, Mr. Gabber?" I asked as he approached.

Jeb looked at his brother and they both laughed.

"Why, hell, we told you this is triple-distilled," he said, climbing up the steps and holding the jar out to me. "Smooth as sanded wood."

I looked dubious as I took it, holding it up into the sunlight. Still playing the big-city tenderfoot, a character they seemed to enjoy, I squinted at the jar, turning it one way and then another.

Finally, Jube bit. "Looking for something?" he asked.

I shrugged, setting the jar on the wooden railing of the porch. "I don't know. I guess if there were any foreign objects or rocks or anything else, they'd all be dissolved by now."

Knowing there was a fine line between kidding and criticism, I hoped I wasn't laying it on too thick, but they laughed again and I knew I was all right.

"I do appreciate it, gentlemen," I said, taking on a serious tone. "You have the reputation for distilling the best whisky in the entire Ozark Mountains, and it's an honor to buy your product. What do I owe you?"

Jube told me there would be no charge, "you being such a good sport and all," and I had thanked them both and turned to go when I heard his brother exclaim, "Well, I'm damned if it ain't old man Black!"

My hair stood up at that. Turning toward the gate, I saw Black shaking a big gunny sack over the fence. Even at that distance, I could see twisting and slithering and I knew he was emptying a bag of snakes onto the Gabbers' property. In just a few seconds, he'd gotten back on his horse and turned it around. He was all bent over in the saddle, like he was in pain, but he felt good enough to turn the horse toward the house, pull up the reins, and point at me before galloping off. When the horse reared and turned, Black's hat fell off. He didn't stop to pick it up.

"Damn," I said. "I'm sorry. I didn't mean to bring any trouble to you."

"That old fool ain't broke the rules like this in a long time," Jube said. "Guess he wants you that bad. But you don't need to worry. Look yonder."

As he pointed to a place on the driveway about halfway between the house and the yard, I saw the pigs, gathering up again. They were acting real strange, standing around looking at the two big black boars, who were grunting, harsh and sharp. It was like they were telling the others what to do. In a moment, all the pigs scampered out of the drive and – yeah, I know how this sounds – lined up on either side. The gravel drive down to the gate was clear and I could see the grass undulating at the far end. A couple of snakes slithered onto the driveway. Damned if I couldn't hear their rattles, echoing dustily in the summer air.

Then it hit me: those damn pigs were making a lane for the snakes to come and get me. I'd been suckered into getting killed. Hell, the Gabbers were probably in cahoots with Old Man Black and his idiot sons!

Without thinking, I vaulted down the steps to the sidecar and jerked out my H&R .22 revolver, knowing that it probably wouldn't be able to kill every snake that was headed my way. But I damn sure was going to get a few, and maybe a Gabber or two!

All of a sudden, Mrs. Gabber was at my side, softly touching my arm. "You don't need that," she said softly. "Just watch."

John, I didn't know what the hell to think. If these people were on Old Man Black's side, I was screwed, with rattlers in front of me and unfriendly hill-billies, probably armed, behind me.

At that point I figured I didn't have much choice but to put my trust in the Gabbers.

About the time I made that decision, all hell broke loose. One of those big boars let out a steamship whistle of rage and charged down the drive, right toward those slithering reptiles. I heard the snap of big jaws and the broken body of a rattler flew up, twisting in its death throes.

Then all the pigs – even more, it seemed, than the ones that had flocked around me when I opened the gate – tore off down the driveway. They burst out of the bushes, ran out from under the house, all of them headed toward the gate where, now, both big boars snapped and grunted, throwing snakes right and left. There was screaming everywhere, just like human screams, when those pigs and snakes met. Soon, the air above the combatants was loud with porcine battle cries and thick with pieces of snake, pigs snapping at them like crocodiles.

I don't know where the thought came from, but it hit me that if old Dante had seen this, his hell would've looked a lot different.

Then, just like that, it was over. The bristled-up boars snuffed a time or two, rooting around in the carnage and occasionally coming up with something chewy. The others nosed around a little bit, too, gulping down pieces of snake. After a couple of minutes, they quietly began to disperse, headed back to wherever they'd come from.

"I... have never seen anything like that," I said, after a few moments. "Never." I looked down at the pistol in my hand. The trembling was almost imperceptible, but it was there.

"Yeah, our pigs are pretty good fighters," said Jeb from behind me.

"Here," said Mrs. Gabber. She held out a Mason jar, smaller than the one sitting on the railing, with about a finger of liquid at the bottom. I knew what it was, and I gratefully threw it down anyway. Maybe I was just getting used to it, but it didn't seem to burn quite as much and after it spread through me it sure as hell steadied my nerves.

"Thanks," I said, handing the jar back.

Then, to Jeb, “Will your pigs die because of this? I mean, from eating rattlers?”

“Naw,” he said. “Couple may be off their feed a day er two. That’s all. Might die if they got bit, but likely they won’t.”

“Fat soaks up the poison,” added Jube. “Hell, they love snakes. One of ‘em crawls onto th’ place, it’s gone in a flash. Even rattlers. So all Black did was give our pigs some good eatin’.”

Up until then, I’d never known that pigs ate snakes. Then again, up until then I’d never met the Gabber boys’ porkers.

My nerves were steady now, and I felt that it was time to end the visit. Besides, there was something on the other side of the fence that I wanted to see. So I said my farewells, secured my gun and the ‘shine in the sidecar, and took off down the gravel drive. It was so slick with blood and gore that I almost slid off it a couple of times before I could get to the gate. I passed a couple of straggler pigs, smaller ones, that were staggering around a little, kind of disoriented. I found myself hoping they wouldn’t die.

Right outside the fence was where I found it. Old Man Black’s hat. My heart sang at that. The cigarette butt seemed to be working, but having an article of clothing was even better. Or so the book told me. Plus, he would know I had it, and that would make him worry.

It was an ugly damn hat, I’ll tell you that. Big and black, sweat-stained, dusty, with down-turned brim and a snakeskin band that I knew had to be rattler. I stuffed it into the sidecar and headed for home.

I don't mean to be cryptic about the cigarette butt and the hat, but it requires some explanation. I was going to give it to you in this letter, but I've gone on and on and it'll wait until next time. Just know that if you hadn't been good enough to send those books to me, it probably wouldn't have happened and I would be in the soup.

Your pal and faithful comrade,

Oink Oink Brown

DODD GENERAL HOSPITAL
Main and Jackson Harrison, Arkansas
June 27, 1939

Dear Mr. Wooley:

I have been asked by Robert Brown to write you. He is in our hospital in Harrison after having been bitten by a rattlesnake and brought here by Dr. Chavez of Mackaville. I must tell you that his condition is so serious that we fear he may not live.

Robert insisted I contact you. His last words before lapsing into a coma were that I should ask you to help his parents if anything happens to him. I have telephoned them and informed them of all that has happened and what we are doing for him. I advised his father against trying to come out here.

We will know soon if he is going to make it. I cannot be too hopeful, and I advise you to be prepared for the worst. Although optimism is not realistic at this point, prayer may be the best thing you can do for him.

Robert has been comatose for the last 10 hours and has only a small chance of regaining consciousness. I will keep you informed of further developments.

Please contact me if I can be of any further assistance.

Sincerely,

Perry P. Jennings, M.D. Dodd General Hospital

3-4242 telephone

563 office number in Harrison

ACKNOWLEDGMENTS

We extend our deepest thanks to Lara Bernhardt, Steven Wooley, Ray Riethmeier, and Bill Bernhardt for their time, insight, observations, and expertise.

ABOUT THE AUTHORS

Robert A. Brown has spent most of his working life in public education, serving as both a reading specialist and a principal, but he has also authored several nonfiction pieces dealing with the Great Depression and its popular culture, including western movies and the so-called "Spicy" magazines of the period. His work includes a piece on the legend of cowboy-movie star Tom Mix commissioned by the National Cowboy and Western Heritage Museum. An internationally known collector of nostalgic items such as movie paper, radio premiums, and pulp magazines, Brown supplied the art and wrote the text for Kitchen Sink Press's popular trading card series *Spicy: Naughty '30s Pulp Covers* and *Spicy: More Naughty '30s Pulp Covers*, which quickly became sold-out collector's items.

Brown initiated what became *The Cleansing*, writing letters on authentic period stationery to his old friend Wooley, using his deep knowledge of the 1930s to portray himself as the WPA employee beset by rural horrors who became *The Cleansing*'s protagonist.

John Wooley made his first professional sale in the late 1960s, placing a script with the legendary *Eerie* magazine. He's now in his sixth decade as a professional writer, having written three horror novels with co-author Ron Wolfe, including *Death's Door*, which was one of the first books released under Dell's Abyss imprint and was also nominated for a Bram Stoker Award. His solo horror and fantasy novels include *Awash in the*

Blood, *Ghost Band*, and *Dark Within*, the latter a finalist for the Oklahoma Book Award.

Wooley is also the author of the critically acclaimed biographies *Wes Craven: A Man and His Nightmares* and *Right Down the Middle: The Ralph Terry Story*. He has co-written or contributed to several volumes of Michael H. Price's Forgotten Horrors series of movie books and co-hosts the podcast of the same name. His other writing credits include the 1990 TV film *Dan Turner, Hollywood Detective* and several documentaries, notably the Learning Channel's *Hauntings Across America*. Among the comics and graphic novels he's scripted are *Plan Nine from Outer Space*, the authorized version of the alternative-movie classic, as well as the recent collections *The Twilight Avenger* and *The Miracle Squad*.